After the Earthquake

Lindasue Flores

ISBN 978-1-936352-56-2
1-936352-56-7

Published by Mirror Publishing
Milwaukee, WI 53214
www.pagesofwonder.com

Printed in the USA

This book is dedicated to the students of Shelton High School as a thank-you for teaching me what young adults like to read.

ACKNOWLEDGEMENTS

I have a great debt of gratitude to Daniel Scott for being my technical editor and giving me encouragement. I wish to thank my husband for giving me advice and putting up with my constant discussions of the book. I thank Brooke Monfort for advice and encouragement.

I also want to thank those at Mirror Publishing for their expertise and professionalism. I especially want to thank Bridget Rongner for polishing the manuscript and Shannon Ishizaki for being so much help.

Chapter 1-Kicked Out

Eighteen-year-old Adam Bennett put the key in the lock, and it clicked open. That is when he discovered that something seemed wrong. The house was quiet. Very quiet. He tried to remember exactly what his mother had said to him. She'd asked him to watch the kids after he got off work, and he'd told her that he worked until twelve that night. He wracked his brain as he stepped into the house. He had told her, hadn't he? The television should have been on. His dad usually watched late night shows on TV on Friday nights and over the weekend, but tonight the house was dead quiet. Spooky quiet.

Surely his parents hadn't left the kids alone . . . on a Friday night? Did they? Adam could imagine his mother failing to inform his father. Why couldn't they have gotten someone to watch the kids? Adam locked the door behind him and went up the stairs as fast as he could. He opened the door to Leila's room. There she was . . . asleep. She had Luke dressed in the pajamas that were covered with little sailboats on a light blue background. He slept in her arms. Leila must have gotten Luke ready for bed herself since their parents had not been there. Quietly, Adam picked up Luke and carried him to his room.

He laid Luke, his six-year-old brother, on the bed and covered him with the blankets on the bed. He couldn't help ruffling the curly blonde, short hair with his hand. Adam glanced at his watch, realizing that the kids had been alone now for hours. Adam didn't think it was a very good idea, and he wasn't even a parent. His twelve-year-old sister was a responsible child, but she wasn't an adult.

She looked like her mother--fit and trim with long, golden-blonde hair. What if someone crazy had tried to break into the house? That had happened in their neighborhood before. What if the kids just got scared and needed an adult? What if one of them got sick?

Adam had really been disgusted with his parents lately.

He was glad he was eighteen, and he looked forward to being on his own. Adam's mother just agreed with whatever his dad said, whether it was right or not. It had been getting in the way lately with his relationship with his mother. He'd always been close to her, and they'd usually provided support for each other against Xander, Adam's dad. Not anymore.

Out of habit, Adam opened the refrigerator and glanced inside even though he wasn't really hungry. He had eaten some of the pizza at work. He'd worked at the Olympic Bowling Alley for two years, and that is how he planned to pay his way through college. Adam had already applied at the University of Washington, and they accepted his application. His dad had a fit and informed him right off that he wasn't paying for him to go to school.

"After all," he said, "I am doing fine and I never went to no high-toned school."

Adam could still remember that day. He thought his dad would have been proud of the fact that he'd been accepted into the U. He would never forget how he felt when he got his acceptance letter and how his father's biting, harsh words felt. Adam had stapled the letter to the wall in his bedroom. Even if he didn't have the money to go there for a while, he was still proud of his acceptance. He hadn't given up. He would just put off going to the university for a couple of years. He planned to work and attend the community college. That way, he wouldn't have nearly as much money to pay back.

His dad still refused to help him with school, like other dads did, but Adam was allowed to live at home while he went to school. His parents, in return, expected him to help out with the kids. The way Adam saw it, they made him their free baby-sitter.

Thinking about his dad, Adam noticed the beer in the refrigerator. His dad wouldn't like it if he opened and drank a beer, but he decided it would help him relax a bit, so he opened up the can. What could his dad do? He was eighteen and not a kid. Adam grinned.

He decided to wait until his parents got in, and then he was going to talk to them about his responsibilities. He had agreed to watch the kids anytime he wasn't working. That had been the deal. In return, he could live at home while working and attending school.

He sat down on the couch, leaned back like he'd seen his dad do, and popped open the beer while he clicked on the television. He spilled a little on his favorite red shirt, but he didn't care. He wasn't really watching the TV. He wasn't even a television-watching kind of person, but it was company. He had never thought about it before, but he, himself, didn't like the house empty. He would never admit that to anyone, though.

To Adam's relief, he saw the headlights of his parents' car through the window. At least, he hoped it was his parents. He thought of the kids. Being alone for so long, they must have really been spooked. Thank goodness Leila had gotten Luke asleep. *He is such a crybaby*, Adam thought.

He sat on the couch listening for his parents to come in while he pretended to be absorbed in watching television.

He heard the key in the lock, and his mother stepped into the room, followed by his dad. "What the heck do you think you are doing with my beer?" his dad said. "Just because you are eighteen doesn't mean you can help yourself to anything that is mine."

Adam had expected that reaction. Maybe he had even opened the beer just to antagonize his father. After all, it was his father who had messed up tonight, not Adam. Maybe that is why he'd gotten the beer. What could his dad do anyway? Adam was just waiting for his chance to tell them what he thought about them leaving the kids.

"You left the kids alone, and I told you, Mom, that I had to work until midnight tonight."

"You didn't tell me, Adam."

"Then you should have called me and waited until I could get home before you left."

His dad said, "The deal was that you could stay here if you contributed by watching the kids for us when we went out. If you aren't going to do that, then you can go stay somewhere else."

"What about my job? You know sometimes on weekends I work late. That is how I'm going to pay for my school. You said you aren't, remember?"

His father answered him, "I got by without college, and you can too. No grown son of mine is going to sit in school all day doing nothing. I can get you a job where I work, and you can pay for your own rent." His father stretched his tall--six-foot-two--slender frame as much as he could as if to intimidate Adam.

Adam had heard it all before. He knew how much he'd hate to work on construction and do that all day every day. He wanted to be the one to plan out the roads. He was interested in making bridges or buildings. He set the beer down on the table and told his dad, "You can have your old beer. I'll get my own. I'll be out in two weeks. I can't wait."

"Not so fast, young man. You have to apologize to your mother for forgetting to tell her that you were working, and you need to take the beer into the kitchen. We're not your servants."

Adam's fury got the best of him, and he clenched his fist. "I have nothing to apologize for!" He turned and smashed his fist into the wall between the supports. Plaster scattered everywhere. He grabbed the beer with his other hand, ran up the stairs toward his room, and slammed the door as hard as he could. They didn't need his room anyway. What was their hurry?

Adam sat down heavily on his bed and continued sipping his beer. He could see his own reflection in the mirror. He had the same blonde, curly hair as his brother. He was about the same height as his father, but thank goodness he looked nothing like him. He was so angry, he was sure he'd be awake all night. He wished his mom wasn't so mealy-mouthed. She hadn't stood up for him at all. Adam was glad that he had to work the next day during Leila's birthday party.

He had to find another place to live. He wasn't sure where to look for somewhere to live, but he would find out. He'd ask around at work the next day.

Chapter 2 - Birthday Party

Adam stood outside his home, almost shaking with anger. Balloons were everywhere, expensive signs formed banners, and a special type of play equipment had been rented. The tacky display was just a bit too elaborate An inflatable jump house and oversized clown from Sweeney's Inflatable Fun had been set up in the front yard. Adam saw that the house was filled with twelve and thirteen-year-old children playing and talking among the birthday banners that hung from the walls. When Adam entered the house, he tossed the package he'd picked up for Leila on top of the obscene pile of packages. He glanced at his mother, then his father. He was furious with both of them.

They had grown used to his anger over the years. Adam knew that he had a hot temper, but when he came to his father with plans for college and a request for financial help, he had tried to be mature and levelheaded. He really had a plan!

But before he had a chance to show his dad how much college meant to him, his dad had simply raised his palm toward Adam and said, "That's stupid."

Adam's father told him--for the hundredth time--how he had been kicked out of his house when he was seventeen and had to make his own way in the world.

Adam had tried to reason with his father, but his attempt at communication quickly turned to anger when his father simply said, "I turned out fine, and you can too if you get your act together."

They hadn't let Adam's plans stop them from having an elaborate birthday party for Leila. If they couldn't afford to help him with college, how could they put on such an elaborate birthday party?

Adam, at eighteen, realized that if he wanted to go to school, then

9

he'd have to find his own way and work to pay his tuition.

He got himself some birthday cake and sat watching the birthday celebration in a rather detached manner as he sipped some punch between taking bites of birthday cake. He made sure he looked at his dad every now and then, giving him a mean expression every chance he got. He wanted his dad to get the message of his anger.

Xander tried not to let Adam spoil his own enjoyment of the birthday party. Secretly, he felt that his son wouldn't make it in college anyway, and Adam's behavior toward the birthday party made a fine example of why he'd have trouble in school.

He and his wife, Claire, had spent a lot of money on Leila, but it felt good to make his daughter so happy. He grinned as he watched Leila's smiling, happy face. He turned away from Adam's rude stares and watched the children having a great time, knowing that he had paid for the party. Claire had ordered the cake, rented playground bouncing equipment, and arranged all of the decorations. What they did with their time and money was none of Adam's business. He paid the bills, not Adam. He had been pondering all of this when the radio came on, and they all heard the stunning news.

"The United States has been taken over by the Democratic Latin Alliance through a well-orchestrated coup that cost less than one hundred American lives and only one Central American life. That person is now considered a martyr for the Alliance." Xander, Claire, Adam, and the children were stunned as the breaking news came over the radio, interrupting the music.

"The Democratic Latin Alliance is taking back the land that was lost in the Spanish-American War as well as more land for revenge and interest in their lost land. Xavier Castollizar is now the president of the Democratic Latin Alliance, which now goes from the Atlantic to the Pacific Ocean and from all of Central America to the Canadian border."

It sounded like a joke. It couldn't be true! The United States was the most powerful nation in the world! *Was*--not anymore? What was going on?

The voice on the interrupted radio station droned on, "All broadcasts will be in Spanish in 30 days, and the only landholders will be people who are of Latin American descent and can prove it! Someone will come to your house in the next 30 days and ask for proof of Latin ancestry. If you have no proof, you will begin paying rent to the

Democratic Latin Alliance. Proof will consist of naturalization papers, birth certificates, or some form of ancestry.

"If you already pay rent, the Democratic Latin Alliance government will be your new landlord unless the owner of your rental property can prove his Latin heritage. When government officials come to your house, you can discuss your papers with them. If you don't know the Spanish language now, you might want to consider learning it because it is the official language of the Democratic Latin Alliance. After 30 days, there will be no more English broadcasts on television or radio. All public broadcasting stations are now owned by the Alliance and will be administered by them. Our new republic reaches from Central America to Canada and from the Atlantic Ocean to the Pacific Ocean. The Democratic Latin Alliance is now the largest and greatest nation in the world."

The birthday party was over. Everyone quietly left as parents came to pick up their children. They were all stunned.

Two weeks after the radio broadcast, a man came to their house. He made them all nervous. He was tall and intimidating with a somber expression on his face and a slight hint of a mustache. His speech was hard to understand, and he used few words.

"What do we need to prove our heritage?" Adam's father asked.

The man responded in clipped words, "A birth certificate from a country in the Alliance or naturalization papers showing you came from there originally."

"And if we don't have either of those?"

"Then you will pay rent to the Democratic Latin Alliance. According to my papers, the rent on this home is $895 per month."

"But we own this house! It is our retirement savings!" Xander said, angry, but guarded.

"That's not my problem or the Democratic Latin Alliance's problem! I return in two weeks. I collect rent."

The man left immediately as the Bennett family sat stunned in their living room. "I'll never pay them a cent!" Xander said.

"What can we do?" Claire answered. She looked at Xander, her expression pained and questioning.

They looked at each other for several minutes with each one deep in thought. Adam's father then looked at each of his children and said, "We'll take a permanent hiking trip. Years ago, I ran into a real large rock cave that had water running into it at the front. We could take some things there and just hang out until all of this blows over. It could be like an extended camping trip. Then, we'll come back and get us another house. I really don't think it will take very long. This supposedly new government will self-destruct rapidly. People won't stand for it."

Adam said, "That sounds a bit extreme to me. If it will only be for a while, why not just stay where we are, and do what they want?"

"We can't just walk away from our own home," Claire said.

"Do you have any better ideas? Because I will not pay these bullies one dime" Xander stared at Claire until she meekly looked down. "Does anyone have any ideas?" He was met with silence. "We'll hike into the mountains and store our food in that cave I found. That is, if I can find it again. Those Alliance people will be so busy trying to get rent and deal with everything else, they'll never have time to look for us."

"The Democratic Latin Alliance may have already formulated laws against hoarding or stockpiling, so we have to be careful not to create any suspicion." Adam and his mother started at his father as if he'd just lost his mind. They waited, silently, for him to go on. "Well, here is my plan. Claire, you go to the store and buy any staples you can get. Adam, you do the same thing."

Adam raised his hand out of habit from school, then shrugged and asked, "What do you mean by 'staples?'"

His father thought for a while and answered, "Anything that will keep without a refrigerator. Just don't buy several of any one thing because that will look suspicious. There will probably be spies everywhere." He was remembering Soviet tactics from the Cold War: buy no more than two of any one thing.

"Claire, you go to a store in Seattle, and, Adam, you go shopping right here in Shelton. I'll go shopping in Tacoma. Adam, how much money do you have in cash?"

"I'm not shopping for the family with my money!" Adam yelled. "You don't need to know how much money I have!"

Xander answered back, almost yelling, "If we are going to survive this, we'll have to pool our resources,"

Adam stomped out of the room and heard his mother's voice as he walked out. "I have about $200 in my purse," she said.

He stopped at his door to listen to his father's answer. He could

12

hear his father fingering money from his wallet.

"I have only $350. I'll get us some batteries, candles, and a few things like that. Leila and Luke, you guys pack all of your warm clothes. You can take only two of your favorite toys. It would be better if they aren't things that need batteries. Make sure you take only your favorite. Pack socks, underwear, coats, and warm clothes. We'll take food later."

Later that night, Adam and his father set off to see whether they could actually find the cave. Their backpacks were as full as they could stuff them with supplies they gathered from the kitchen. They drove silently, neither man interested in conversation. It was close to midnight when Xander drove through the gate to the entrance of the park, but there was no gatekeeper there. It was just as he hoped. He drove as far as the road went, and there was a parking area for hikers to leave their car to follow the hiking trail. Xander always enjoyed hiking and exploring on his own. He usually stuck to the trail until he was well out of sight of people. That night, his only problem was to find the place where he'd veered off of the trail many summers ago when he'd found the cave.

As they walked, Xander became worried he might not find the right place. He thought hard about what the trail had looked like on that day when he had found the cave so long ago. Concentrating hard, he tried to envision the trail as it had been that day. He was confident that he could find the place where a tree had been broken in half right along the trail. The tree had not been blocking the trail, and the rangers always tried to leave the wilderness as it was--untouched by human hands. They walked on, still in silence. What could be said when they were about to lose their home, and they were looking for a cave for replacement?

"Here!" Xander whispered softly to Adam as if an intruder might be there to overhear them.

Adam, mimicking his father's low tone of voice, asked, "Is this the cave?"

"No, this is just where we turn off the trail."

"You always told me to stay on the trail." Adam said curtly.

"If I had, then I wouldn't know where the cave is."

"I'm still not sure that this is the thing to do. Why can't we just pay the rent while things get worked out? The whole mess has got to be some kind of mistake," Adam said, his voice rising.

"Keep your voice down."

"Oh, right, are the bears going to hear us? It is well after midnight, and who do you see?"

Xander, used to Adam's sarcasm, didn't bother to reply. He just kept walking but glanced behind him to make sure that Adam was still following. He was. They walked in silence, and Xander felt himself getting tired. Fatigue had been a battle for him since all of this trouble had started on the day of the birthday party. He was worried.

Finally, he thought he saw the cave. But it appeared much smaller than he remembered. Still, he walked up the trail toward a small indentation in the mountain rock. Sure enough, it was the cave. But in the two years since he had found it, a small bush had grown over the opening. The cave was barely visible. They pushed aside the bush. Xander was careful not to disturb the bush, but Adam carelessly stepped on part of it with his boots. Xander pointed his palm at Adam.

"Get back! Don't disturb that bush! It might be noticed. Just try to use your head," he said.

"You didn't tell me," Adam said, angry again. His dad ignored him. He was just happy that he had actually found the cave, so his annoyance with Adam's clumsiness faded. He had to figure out if it would be possible to hide in the cave for a while. He felt that soon their lives could return to normal anyway. The United States Government always prevailed against its enemies, and it would continue to do so.

Adam and Xander stepped farther into the cave and looked around. Water was dripping close to the front of the cave. Farther back, the cave was dry. The air was damp and smelled musty, but the cave was very large. Perfect! The walls of the cave behind the dripping water were a very hard gneiss rock. Xander pushed away some loose rocks near the side of the cave and created a type of shelf. "Let's unload everything and get back home," he told Adam.

"I'm not going to put my carefully packed things on that dirty old ledge," Adam said with a clipped tone.

"Put them where you want, but empty that backpack because we have to get back before daybreak."

Slowly and reluctantly, Adam unloaded his backpack. His nerves were shattered from a combination of fear and anger--making him want to hit something. Instead, he stomped out of the cave without saying a word.

Xander was tired and had no energy for Adam and his tirades, so he just followed him out. He stayed behind Adam to see where he went, and just as he thought Adam was walking in the wrong direction, Xander hurried ahead and headed toward the car. He was going home, and Adam could stay or go. Adam changed his direction to follow his father. He didn't say a word. They got to the vehicle and Adam stayed silent. He slammed the door as hard as he could.

"You know, Adam, if you break that door, we won't be able to fix it, and it could cause us a great deal of trouble," Xander said.

Adam shouted back, "I've got my own car. I don't care!"

Dawn was just breaking as they arrived back home. Both men were tired and went inside to lie down. "Call in sick for me," Xander told Claire.

Xander slept until late afternoon. When he got up, he got together more supplies and put them into his backpack for another trip to the cave. He went into Adam's room to get him up, but Adam refused. "Leave me alone! I'll go up in my own car with my own backpack," he said, stretching his arms and shutting his eyes. He then rolled away from his dad.

"Fine, but you can't leave Leila and Luke alone," his father told him.

"I'm eighteen! I can do what I want!"

Xander turned and left the room. He didn't have the time or the inclination to deal with Adam and his temper. "Suit yourself. No one wants to be around you anyway."

Xander and Claire took their own backpacks, as well as Leila and Luke's, and climbed into the car. They drove quietly and peacefully to the turnaround, then got out of the car.

"I am so tired of trying to deal with Adam," Xander told his wife. The stress their family was going through was beginning to show. He continuously glanced right and left as if looking for danger on both sides of the road.

Claire worried about the children's future and what might happen in the months to come. "That is why Adam has such a temper. It is a habit with him because he acts just like you!" she said.

"Oh, so now Adam's behavior is all my fault?"

"You sure haven't helped one bit!" Claire said. "He has no consequences when he talks back. He just gets away with it."

Xander answered her, "I just want peace. That is all."

15

They walked on. The backpacks were getting heavier and heavier as they walked. Claire had trouble keeping up with Xander. She had always enjoyed hiking, but Xander was in better shape. With sweat pouring off her face, Claire glanced up toward Xander. He was quite a ways ahead of her, but she didn't want to ask him to take a breather. She knew he felt uptight by the way he stomped while walking.

"He's blaming me for something!" Claire said softly to herself. Then he disappeared--just like that! Claire stopped frozen in her tracks. Her breathing quickened as panic began to overtake her. She jumped as Xander suddenly reappeared, without the backpacks, from an opening in the mountainside. The cave!

He hurried to Claire to get the two backpacks she had carried up the hill. She was glad to be rid of them and followed him into the small entrance to the cave.

"Walk around the bushes because they help keep the cave entrance hidden."

Claire didn't question him. She just stepped around the bush and into a very large cave. Xander was already headed toward the back to unload the packs. He paid no attention to what was in them. They'd get to that later. Right then, he was concentrating on getting as much into that cave as possible. They had a week and a half left.

"Let's head back quickly, so maybe I can get some sleep. I need to show up at work so that nothing looks suspicious. You guys can load the packs again tomorrow," he said as he walked toward the cave entrance. "We need one more day for nonfood items. Then, we can pack food to take."

He's right, Claire thought to herself. *We have to plan carefully. I don't want to pay any money to that fake government either. Not one dime.*

She asked Xander, "Do you think we can pull this off?"

"I think we can, and I think we'll only have to stay here about a month. I think the Democratic Latin Alliance will implode on its own. The U.S. will probably be a shambles afterward, but we can build it back up." Any shift from one government to another could be disastrous--as history has already proven.

They got back to the car, threw in the empty backpacks, and drove off. "See if you can get Adam to make a trip up tomorrow night, will you?"

"Do all the trips have to be at night?

"I think all of them except the last one. When we leave for the last time, we'll leave early--just at daybreak."

They drove home in silence. Stress was beginning to show its ugly face, and it made everyone edgy. Xander entered the house and went to bed. Claire went to Adam's room to ask him to make a run to the cave with some supplies. She knocked on his door softly, hoping to keep from agitating him. Claire had learned to avoid Adam's temper just as she had learned to avoid Xander's temper.

"Come in," Adam said groggily.

"Adam, will you go up to the cave and take a load of clothing and stuff? It can be anytime today." Claire almost whispered this request.

Yawning in an exaggerated way, Adam rolled over on his bed to face Claire. "Only if you'll give me gas money. If I'm running an errand for you, then you should give me gas money," he told her. He smiled, sure that he was demonstrating mature actions.

"Then maybe I'll charge you for your supper then."

"Fine! I'll buy my own supper!" Adam said. "Don't even set a place for me."

Claire, tired of Adam's attitude, slammed the door as she walked out. After thinking about the necessity of Adam making a run to the cave, she dug out two twenty dollar bills and returned to his room.

Adam was sorry he'd talked to his mother that way. He felt he'd make it up to her. Then, she reappeared with the two twenty dollar bills.

I'll spend the entire forty dollars on materials for the cave, even if I don't believe in the idea, he thought.

Adam felt that everything would eventually clear up and that this whole cave thing was a stupid exaggeration like the birthday party. For his mother's--not his father's--sake, he'd act like he was agreeing with the idea; and for himself, he would treat the cave as an adventure. He dressed and left the house and then decided he'd go to Tacoma. He thought he'd get a better idea of what was really happening instead of just listening to the radio and his dad.

On his way to the shopping center, Adam saw a group of U.S. Army tanks and Humvees in an empty lot. He recognized the tanks as American tanks, but the men in and around them did not wear U.S. Army uniforms. Their uniforms were red with white lettering. The

17

letters were *DLA*. To see those letters on red uniforms of men with U.S. equipment was alarming. Maybe his dad was right. At least, about something. He went to the shopping center and noted that several businesses were closed. Then, in front of one store was a large sign saying: "NO HOARDING."

He went toward the grocery store and saw another sign: "LOOTERS WILL BE SHOT!"

This alarmed Adam, and he drove on to the larger super mart. Two armed guards, also with red uniforms with the white letters *DLA*, stood just inside the door. They were heavily armed. More nervous than ever, he grabbed a cart and decided the first thing he'd get was a large trash can so that food could be stored away from the animals in the forest. Who knows, the cave just might be a good hide-out when he got sick and tired of the crap his parents--especially his father--dished out to him.

The first thing Adam put in his cart was a trash can--the kind with wheels so that he could drag it up the mountain. It would be awkward to get up it, but he was strong. Stretching to his full six foot height and flexing his muscles a little bit to feel their strength, Adam placed the trash can in his cart. He subtracted the cost of the trash can from what he had, then realized that it cost more than he'd thought it would--close to thirty dollars--and he had more things to buy. Maybe it wouldn't be so important after all. Adam put the plastic can back to give himself time to reconsider.

He walked around the store looking for items that might be useful. Adam tried to picture in his mind what they had used on previous camping trips. He picked up some batteries for the boom box that he never used (he had an I-pod). He had decided if he did spend some time in the cave, he'd need music. Then, he got some beans and macaroni.

As he went through the store, he noticed that several items were missing, and there were bare spots on the shelves. He'd never seen that before. He decided to get a flashlight and some first-aid supplies. When he realized there were only two packages of Band-Aids left, he got them both.

He picked up some matches, then decided to get a few candles. The only candles left were some expensive scented candles, so he got two. He took two of the last remaining six-packs of pop. Finally, Adam went back to the trash container and put it on top of his cart. He had realized that he'd have a problem carrying all of his supplies in his backpack, and the trash container would come in handy.

He handed his debit card to the clerk, and she refused it. "I'm sorry, but we can only take cash," she said.

Adam was shocked. He barely had enough cash. There was only a ten-dollar bill left for gas money. Adam was glad that his mother had given him the two twenty-dollar bills. Otherwise, he wouldn't have had enough money.

"What do you need the trash can for?" the clerk asked.

Adam felt himself getting a bit testy, but he remained guarded. "I'm helping my dad clean up," he said.

He wondered, *Why the questions? Clerks don't ask questions about what you buy.* While the clerk packaged the items, Adam thought, *Maybe dad is right, and things are worse than I had thought. Could it really take a while for the government to get back to normal?*

"Just put everything into the trash container," he told the cashier.

The trash can barely fit into Adam's car even with the front seat pushed back as far as he could get it. He bought gas, drove out of the city, and finally headed toward the Hoh National Forest. Just as he was getting comfortable, there was a roadblock right in the middle of the road. The officials again were using U.S. Army vehicles, and they had on the red uniforms with the initials *DLA* across the right shoulder. They acted unfriendly, and it made Adam nervous.

One man, the taller and huskier one, walked up to Adam's car and asked, in very brief, clipped tones, "What do you have in the car?"

Adam gave the same answer he'd given the clerk at the store, "Some cleaning things that I'm going to use to help my dad with the yard."

The man questioned further, "Where are you going?"

Adam answered, "Home, so that I can work on the yard." Two or three of the uniformed men conferred with each other, then they let Adam through. Adam was glad that they didn't open the trash can. They had only glanced through the windows, but it was enough to make him nervous.

He drove on toward the forest, and he found the forest service road that his dad had shown him. Driving all the way to the end of the road, Adam found the little turnaround and was grateful that no one was around. He hadn't expected anyone, but he was glad that nothing further had gone wrong.

The hike to the cave started out easy, but as he dragged the trash can up the hill, the walk got a little harder than he thought it would be. When he finally made it, Adam found that it was difficult to get the container into the cave opening without bothering the bushes in front of the entrance. He didn't want to disturb the bushes because he liked them, not because his dad had suggested it. To get the container inside, he had to empty it, then squeeze the top and shove it hard.

When he finished, he was finally able to rest. He sat down and opened a can of pop. He was hungry, but he'd told his mother that he'd get his own supper. He didn't find anything that could be eaten, and he wished that he had gotten more food. He'd have to go home and make himself a sandwich, but it would take him a while to get there. He took his pop and walked back to his car.

When he got home, he snuck into the side of the house, made himself a quick peanut butter and jelly sandwich, and quietly went up the stairs toward his room. By then, it was 7:00 in the evening.

"You kids come here a minute, and bring along your empty backpacks please." Xander yelled up the stairs. Leila and Luke came along with Adam down the stairs. "We have only a week left of our two weeks," Xander told the children. "We've got to be out of our house before then."

"Personally," Adam said, "I think it would be better to stay here than to try to run away."

"You don't know anything about it," Xander told him. Both men were squaring off, ready for a fight. "Your safety is my responsibility."

"Not mine," Adam answered back. "I'm eighteen, and I am plenty capable of taking care of myself."

"Let's just get on with it and not argue," Claire said. "I want you guys to hand me your empty backpacks, and I'll fill up each one with food. While I'm filling the packs, you guys go to your rooms, and put on all the clothes you can manage. Start with underwear, then your Levis, and then your sweats. Put on as much as possible. Get on all of the T-shirts and sweaters you can. Then, get your two favorite blankets, and put one on each arm by folding it the long way. It will feel awkward, but it won't take long to get to the cave."

"Only for you, Mom. I'll do as you ask," Adam said as he raised his eyebrows toward his father. Adam put his arm around Leila's shoulder and said, "Come on, guys. Let's do as Mom asked us." He deliberately omitted referring to his father.

Xander stomped toward his own bedroom. Claire gathered up all five of the packs and carried them toward the kitchen. She had a plan, and she knew just what she'd do. She'd put one jar of peanut butter and one jar of jam in each pack and finish by putting in anything else she could cram into them. She packed Luke's bag first. She felt that he couldn't handle the heavier items. She put in dried beans, packaged, dried mashed potatoes, and some dried fruit. When she finished with Luke's bag, she set it down on the floor and began loading up Leila's bag. When she finished Leila's bag, she had only three more to fill up. It wouldn't be long before they'd be on their way. It would be another long night. Claire hoped that this whole scenario was really necessary. She didn't completely agree with Xander, but she wasn't in the habit of contradicting him. Mostly she agreed with Adam--that they should just wait it out and let the politicians and the Army work things out.

Chapter 3 - Narrow Escape

Claire set down Leila's full bag and picked up Adam's just as the doorbell rang. Her heart jumped a beat, and she began shaking. No one they knew would come to the house at this time of night. Who could it be?

"I'll get the door," Adam yelled. Out of some unfamiliar fear, Claire grabbed the packs and stuffed all of them under the sink. She was glad that not all of them were full. Just as she finished, two armed men, followed by Xander, came to the kitchen door.

They acted strange. "What are you doing in here?" The taller one asked.

She looked at the two men dressed in red uniforms with the letters *DLA* on their left shoulders and wielding guns. Claire was more frightened than she'd ever been in her life. Behind the center kitchen island, her legs shook.

"Why are there so many things stacked on the cabinet?" the second man questioned.

"I got groceries today, and I haven't had time to put things away yet." Claire told them. She tried her best to sound matter-of-fact instead of scared to the bones.

They stood at the entrance to the kitchen. The tall one lowered his gun. "Everything belongs to the Democratic Latin Alliance," he said. "There will be no tolerance or dissidence and no varying from daily routine."

To Xander, he said, "There have been reports of strange conduct concerning this household."

"I can't imagine why," Xander told him. He was trying hard to keep his cool and act nonchalant.

"Where are the children?" the tall man with the gun asked.

Claire answered, "They are getting ready for bed. They have school tomorrow."

"Where are their rooms?" he asked.

Claire's legs were shaking even harder, but she still stood behind the kitchen island. "Their rooms are all upstairs," she told them. Both men immediately trooped upstairs. Adam had already gone back up to the top of the stairs and barely had time to duck into Luke's room to help keep him from being so scared.

"Luke, don't answer any questions, okay? If you have to answer any questions, tell them you are getting ready for bed. Drop you jacket and other clothes quickly behind the bed and keep on your sweats," Adam told him softly--barely louder than a whisper.

"Why?" Luke asked.

Adam didn't answer. Instead he put his finger to his mouth to quiet Luke. The men burst into the room.

"What is going on here?" both men questioned. Adam at once recognized the uniforms on the two men--red with white lettering. Then he noticed the gun and tensed with nervousness.

When Luke saw the gun, he started shaking. "We're getting ready for bed," he said. Then he started to cry, so Adam walked toward him and hugged him.

"You are upsetting him at bedtime," Adam said. For some reason, this made him angry, and he felt protective toward Luke for the first time that he could ever remember. "What do you want anyway?" he asked the men. That was when he realized that the men wanted to scare and intimidate them. Maybe Luke's fear would cause the men to be less guarded. Maybe it would make them less suspicious.

The two men walked back down the stairs. Either they didn't know about Leila, or they were satisfied that their investigation was complete.

For the first time since all of it began, Adam realized just how serious things were. Maybe his dad was right after all. Adam was secretly glad that he'd done such a great job today. His dad would be proud of him. Maybe for the first time ever. He stayed where he was, with his arms around Luke, until he heard the front door slam.

"Luke, everything is all right. Just hurry and get ready like Dad asked, okay?" Then Adam went downstairs, taking the steps two at a time with nervous energy.

"What was that about?" he asked his father.

"Son, I really don't know, but finish getting ready, and we'll leave a little more carefully than we had planned. I guess we'll only make one trip tonight after all. They might be watching the house." Adam looked at his mother, who was pulling the backpacks out from under the sink. She turned toward him with tears freely rolling down her cheeks. She did not even try to hide the tears. All of this stress was getting to her too. Adam never saw his mother cry before, and this shook him up.

"It will be okay, Mom," he said.

Xander walked to the living room and carefully pulled back just one little corner of the living room drape as he watched the two men return their guns into the holsters and get into their car. They drove about two blocks, then stopped. Xander stayed frozen at the window, watching. The car pulled up to another house, and he heard a shot fired. It could have been just a warning. It was hard to figure all of this out.

He asked Adam, "How much gas do you have?"

"My tank is full. Why?"

"Because I think we should take your car and have you drive while we lie on the floor. Just as a precaution."

Adam added his next comment tentatively. "Okay, but you have to replace my gas!"

"Whatever," his dad answered. "Go get yourself ready."

Adam put on four pairs of underwear, one pair of pants, and a pair of sweats. He was only able to get on two T-shirts, one regular shirt, and two sweaters. He felt like a stuffed potato.

He grabbed his radio and managed to stuff it in next to his skin by tucking in his T-shirts. They helped the radio stay in place. "No one will know I snuck in this," he said softly, proud of himself for performing another act of noncompliance against his dad. Then he went into Leila's room to see how she was doing. She had on a couple pairs of pants, a couple T-shirts, and a dress. She'd done well, but she was in tears.

"I want to take my teddy bear, but Mom didn't say anything about my teddy bear, and I already have to carry one blanket on each arm."

"Here's what we can do," Adam told her, grinning. "We'll take your teddy bear and stuff it under your dress. That will hold it up. Then we'll put your jacket on over everything."

He grabbed Leila's teddy bear and pushed it under her dress. He barely managed to get it under there, but it worked.

"It feels funny," Leila said.

Adam grinned as he told her, "You just have to make it to the cave. Remember--think of it as another camping trip."

With her eyes glistening with tears, she said, "But what about those men?"

"I don't think we'll see those men again." He was thinking, *At least I hope not.* To Leila, though, he said, "Now, let me get your blankets and fold them so that you can carry one over each arm and go downstairs."

Adam hurried to Luke's room to see how he was doing. He had on two shirts and a pair of sweats over some pants.

"Okay, Luke, you did great. Now, get your jacket on, and I'll help you get your blankets." He folded the blankets, but he couldn't get them to fit on Luke's arms. Instead, he grabbed a couple of sheets and folded them. "I guess you're just going to have to go with a sheet, Luke," Adam told him. "I'll take an extra blanket for you. Now, head downstairs."

As he entered his own room again, Adam went to his bed and folded up two blankets, so they would hang from each arm. He went to his closet and got out another blanket for Luke. He folded the third blanket, put on his jacket, threw the blankets around his arms, and went downstairs. He hoped that the radio hidden under his clothes would not affect his driving. He didn't want to go anywhere without at least this radio. Luke had given it to him last year for Christmas, and Adam had acted like he loved it. In reality, he'd never even turned it on. Now, he wanted to take it to the cave. Maybe that cave could become his own little hideout after everything was settled down.

"Are we ready to go?" Xander asked everyone.

"Wait, I just have to go up and get my blankets," Claire said.

Adam, Leila, and Luke had to put down their blankets before they put on their back packs, but they got them on.

"But it feels yucky!" Luke said.

"We don't have to go far," Xander told him.

"Here's what we are going to do," Xander said. "Each one of you kids go get into the car and lie down on the floor in the back. Your

25

mother and I will get in the trunk. The last person to get into the car will be Adam. All of us will be out of sight except for Adam. He will be driving. When we are away from people, Adam will stop the car, and we can get ourselves comfortable. You are both going to have to stay on the floor, even if you feel crowded. You have to stay hidden. You can put your blankets on the floor and lie on top of them. It will be more comfortable for you that way. We'll only be on the road for about three hours."

Luke and Leila went out to the car first, then Claire and Xander. Adam waited for a little while, then went out to the car, got in, and drove toward town. In town, he made a U-turn and headed toward the Hoh National Forest. Just outside town, they stopped the car at a park-and-ride. Xander moved to the front seat, and Claire sat next to the window in the back with her arm around Luke. Luke leaned affectionately against his mother, and they settled down for the rest of their drive. No one talked, and Adam found himself getting a little sleepy. It was already close to midnight.

"Son, would you like me to drive?" Xander asked. Adam didn't want his father to drive his car, but he glanced back in the car at his mother, with Luke sleeping in her lap, and Leila resting against the door. He didn't want to risk driving off the road.

"Okay, Dad. Thank you."

Xander looked at Adam strangely because it wasn't like Adam to say "thank you." The entire family had been acting strange since all of this happened.

Xander drove on in silence. Claire, Luke, and Leila were all asleep, so when the car stopped, no one wanted to get out in the cold, drizzly October rain.

"We have to get going," Xander said forcefully and a little too loud. Adam was the first out. He got a flashlight from the side of the door and opened the door for Claire. As she got out, Adam helped Luke get out and get all of his things situated for the long hike to the cave.

"Hold it," Xander said softly.

Adam thought he sounded scared. "What is it?"

Xander flashed his flashlight onto the ground. "Look here," he showed Adam. "It looks like someone has gone up the hill with two bikes. Adam, you stay here with Mom and the kids while I go on to see what made those tracks." He stepped forward, then pulled a pistol out of his coat pocket. "Hide behind those bushes until I get back."

"Don't you want me to go with you?" Adam asked.

"No, stay here and help the kids and your mother."

Adam herded Leila and Luke to the bushes that were up a little higher than the car and away from the road. After everyone was well hidden, he went back to the tracks. Something clicked in his mind. Adam remembered. He shined the light on the tracks that had pushed an indentation into the wet leaves. The soft ground had given way to the wheels on his trash can. He went back to the hidden group and told them, "Come on, it's okay."

"Are you sure?" his mother asked him. "We are supposed to wait for Dad."

"Remember the trip I made earlier today? I bought a trash can to put things in, so they'd be safe from the animals." He didn't tell her that he planned on using the cave even after they quit using it as a hideout.

The children were tired, and Adam was exhausted. The climb would be long with the things they had brought. When they were halfway up the mountain, Luke got tired and thought he couldn't go any farther. He started crying. Adam had Leila, Claire, and Luke wait. He could come back after getting rid of his things. His radio was beginning to get uncomfortable under his shirt. As burdened down as he was, he couldn't really help anyone. He went on up the mountain toward the cave.

Just as he was about to enter the cave, he heard a crash as his father yelled, "What the hell is this thing doing here?" He kicked the plastic trash can clear to the end of the cave, even though it was half-full of Adam's purchases.

Adam awkwardly stepped into the cave and pulled out his radio. "I bought that today to use for food storage," Adam proudly told him.

"We don't need crap like that!" Xander yelled. "What were you thinking? Where is your mother?"

"She is about halfway down the mountain with Luke and Leila," Adam told him with a soft, deflated voice. The one thing he thought his dad would be happy that he had done instead only made him mad.

"Wouldn't you know it," Adam spoke, mostly to himself. He thought about the kids and threw down his backpack and blankets. He peeled off most of his extra clothes and went out of the cave to help the others. He just turned his back on his dad because he didn't have any energy for an altercation with him just now. It could wait for later. But he would not let it go. He intended to fight back---after he got the kids and his mother up the mountain and unloaded. It didn't take him long to reach them.

"Come on, guys," he said. He picked up Luke and Leila's backpacks. He put one on his back and the other across his shoulder. Then he got their blankets. They trudged up the hill much easier than before. As they went inside, the kids started peeling off their extra clothing. Claire dropped her backpack, peeled off her extra clothing, and dumped out the contents of her backpack.

"You guys wait for us." Xander said as he took Claire's arm and headed out the cave. "I'm going to smooth out those tracks, and we are going to get back to town and pack some more things. We'll be back sometime in the early afternoon in my car. Just stay inside the cave, bed down, and sleep for a while. One more trip will be the most we can afford to try to pull off. After that, we will not be able to go back to the house. I don't want the kids at the house anymore at all. I don't want anyone thrown in jail or whatever they might do to us. We can't run that risk."

"But what about my gas?" Adam asked.

Xander, disgusted, looked at Adam, and made hard fists with both of his hands. Claire gave him one of "those looks," so he just reached into his pocket, pulled out his billfold, grabbed a ten-dollar bill, and tossed it on the ground. Silently, he and Claire walked out of the cave and down the mountain.

Adam picked up the bill and sat down, deflated.

Leila began crying, "I want to go with Mom and Dad."

Adam looked at her, and affection overtook his anger as he hugged her. "They'll be back. I'll tell you what, how would you like a pop?"

"Where would you get a pop?"

"Right back here," Adam said.

He hoped that the cans of pop were intact and not leaking over everything after his dad kicked the trash can so hard. Looking for the place where they could get a pop, Luke and Leila followed Adam farther into the cave. Adam tipped over the large trash can, emptying it so that he could retrieve the things inside. Sure enough, one of the cans was spouting pop, but the rest were okay. When he handed Leila a can, she smiled and began drinking.

He also handed Luke a pop.

Luke was so excited, he said, "You are so smart, Adam."

Their gratitude helped him a lot with his dour mood. Adam sat down with his own pop--or what was left of it--in the leaking can. Pop was all over everything. He resisted letting his anger surface as he watched the two tired children.

"I don't want any more pop," Luke said.

"That's okay, but set it up here on this ledge, so you can get some later," he told Luke.

"I'm tired," Leila said.

"Well, let's fix you a pallet so you can rest until Mom and Dad get back, okay?"

Luke looked around in the dark cave and began whimpering. "This place is scary. When will Mom and Dad get back?"

Adam did not know where to start explaining. He didn't know exactly when their mom and dad would be back, but it would be a good six hours. They were going to be living in the cave for a while--until the Government of the United States was back in control. How long would that be? Adam didn't know.

"Leila and Luke, you might as well know right now that when Mom and Dad get back, it will be to stay. Let's figure out a place to make a pallet and rest. Let's pretend we are camping for a very long time."

Leila looked up at Adam. "This place is cold and dark, and it is scary. Luke is right!"

Adam was only used to dealing with the kids at home, where there was a TV and plenty to eat. "Like I said, let's just pretend we are camping." He held up a candle a little higher. "Let's explore and find someplace dry. We'll just get our blankets and take a nap while we wait for Mom and Dad."

Several places in the front of the cave had dripping water, but one side was fairly dry and had a rock ledge.

The area where they could sleep was about the size of a small bedroom, and the rest of the cave was about the size of a large living room with vaulted ceilings. The extra height made the cave seem larger than it really was.

"How about we get our blankets and fix a bed right here?" Adam asked. He didn't wait for the kids to answer. He just headed toward the blankets. Leila and Luke followed him. He handed Luke his mother's blankets and the one he had carried for him.

"Here, Luke, you use Mom's, and keep it warm for her. Leila, you take yours and Dad's, and I'll take mine. We'll all bundle up together and wait for Mom and Dad."

"But, I have to go pee," Luke wailed.

"Me, too, Adam," Leila added.

"You can't pee in the cave. Luke, I'll take you outside with my flashlight, then we'll both pee. I'll come back and help Leila find a spot away from the cave too."

Adam reached for Luke's hand and lead him out of the cave. He hadn't thought about going to the bathroom. He really hadn't thought they'd get this far moving into the cave. It seemed so primitive. Mom and Dad could have just waited until things calmed down instead of going through all of this and scaring the kids. Adam secretly wished that all of this had never happened. But it had!

"You are jerking my arm, and you're going too fast. I can't keep up," Luke whined.

Adam resisted his first instinct to get even more angry. He rotated his flashlight to see more of the ground under their feet and found a cluster of bushes.

"Here, Luke. We can pee here," he said trying to resist lashing out at him.

When they went back to the cave, Adam held Leila's arm and led her out of the cave with the flashlight. They walked in silence toward the cluster of bushes, and Leila spoke quietly to Adam. "This is scary. It is so dark and quiet."

"I'll stand right here, and you can go over there by the bushes."

He handed her the flashlight. "Here, you take the flashlight so that you won't trip. And, remember, pretend you are camping at Cougar Mountain."

She took the flashlight, but hung on to Adam's arm.

"Walk with me until I get to the bushes, and wait for me there." He started to give her a little encouraging push, then she said, "Please?"

He walked with her toward the bushes and waited just on the other side. Leila was incredibly fast in getting back, and he took her arm while they walked silently back to the cave.

They gathered the pile of blankets and went toward the back of the cave where it was dark. Adam used the flashlight only to find them a place to put their bedding.

"You guys go over there with the blankets you can carry, and I'll take the rest."

He flashed the light toward the back of the cave and watched the kids head back. He flashed the light back toward the things piled in a heap closer to the mouth of the cave. He picked up one sheet and the other four blankets and headed toward the back of the cave.

He smoothed down two blankets, then put a sheet over it. "You guys lie down, and I'll cover you up. Leila, you go first, then Luke."

Both Luke and Leila said, "But, you are lying down, too, aren't you?"

He had not intended to lie down, but then he realized just how tired he was, so he said, "I guess so."

All three of them snuggled together, and it really did feel warm and cozy, except that they didn't have any pillows.

"Just a minute," Adam said, and he walked over to the pile and got out each person's coat. He rolled the coats up and gave one to each child. "We'll pretend these are pillows." The rolled-up coats felt very much like pillows, and they fell asleep quickly from fatigue.

Sometime during the night, Adam felt a strong rocking feeling. It only woke him up partially. A couple of hours later, there was a very strong feeling of movement with a loud cracking sound followed by a slow rumble, and it woke up all three of them. Adam wasn't sure whether they should run outside or stay in the cave.

Leila asked, "Is that an earthquake? Shouldn't we be running outside?"

Luke whined, "I'm scared."

Adam told them, "Let's get up and run outside."

All three of them scrambled out of their coverings and ran toward the mouth of the cave. Just as they got to the opening, rocks started falling down from higher up the mountain.

"Wait," Adam said. "We might be hit by the rocks."

Watching the big rocks tumble down the mountain like they were Styrofoam, Leila and Luke held onto Adam. He watched as the rocks fell on top of the bush that his dad had tried so hard to protect. The bush was now under so much debris, all you could see was a few leaves.

The shaking stopped. It just stopped. Adam couldn't help but stare at the place where the bush had been. He wondered if he would get in trouble over it. Then he realized that the cave opening had lost half of its size. It was still large enough for a person to get through, but the trash can would no longer fit through the opening.

He stood frozen, with the two kids hanging onto him, as he peered out of the cave. It was still dark, and the darkness added to the eerie feeling of being inside the cave during an earthquake.

"Let's just go back to bed and wait for Mom and Dad," Adam said, as much to hear his own voice as to address the two kids.

They didn't have the flashlight because they had immediately run to the front of the cave when the shaking began, so Adam held onto Leila, who hung onto Luke's hand, until they felt their way to the back of the cave. As they lay down, Adam wondered whether aftershocks might occur. Leila and Luke fell back asleep as Adam wondered if they should leave the cave. It's what you were supposed to do if you were in a building during an earthquake. You were supposed to get out of the building and away from anything that might come down and hit you. But they weren't in a building. They were in a cave, and Adam had never read anything about what to do during an earthquake if you were in a cave. Wondering about these things, he fell asleep too.

Leila woke up crying. "Adam! Where are Mom and Dad?"

He gathered her in his arms, trying to cradle her against further pain. "I don't know, Leila." He told her. He had expected their parents to return by daybreak. He could now see a tiny bit of daylight coming through the cave opening. Light in the cave was dim because the opening was smaller. He got up and went to the mouth of the cave and peeked out, but he didn't see anything unusual except for the crushed bush with the rock on top of it.

He went back to Leila and told her, "We have no choice but to wait a little longer for Mom and Dad. Try to get back asleep without waking Luke."

Chapter 4 - An Earthquake

Again they felt a major jolt, accompanied by another cracking sound, that lasted for almost a full minute, but seemed like hours.

Luke started crying, "This cave is scary. I don't like it here!"

"Me, neither," said Leila.

They both said, "We want Mom and Dad."

Adam thought for a moment and told them, "Let me check the cave to see how solid it is. I think it is solid rock. You two help me check the sides of the cave. Use your hands and feel along the wall for a crack. We may have to leave, but then we'll have to worry about trees falling on us."

He got up and looked more carefully at the basic structure of the cave. He reached out his hands and tried to get the solid rock to crumble. It didn't. There was very little loose rock and nothing that even remotely felt like a crack. Luke and Leila got up.

"We have to go pee," Luke said as he held his sister's hand.

"Take turns," Adam told them. "Luke, you go first then hurry back."

When Luke returned, Leila went to the bushes. While she was coming back, the ground shook again. She ran toward Adam as fast as she could. They slipped into the mouth of the cave and watched while more rocks rolled past the opening and fell down the mountain.

"It's an aftershock," Adam said.

"I still think we should go outside," Leila said.

"No, this cave is solid. We checked it, remember? I think we are safer here."

33

"I want Mom and Dad," Luke cried. "When are they getting back?"

"I don't know, Luke. I don't know."

"I am hungry," Leila said.

"Well, you get the rest of your soda pop, and I'll look around and see what we can eat while we're waiting for Mom and Dad."

He started rummaging through the irregular piles of things, but all he found was some dried fruit and crackers. Then he remembered the peanut butter and jam. "Well, it looks like we have some dried fruit and peanut butter and crackers."

"But what about breakfast? Mom doesn't let us have peanut butter and crackers for breakfast," Leila said.

"Well, we just have to eat what we have here, don't we? We can't do anything until Mom and Dad get back anyway." They all ate their peanut butter and crackers and nibbled on some of the dried fruit. Afterward, they sipped on the pop.

"Be sure to set your pop down in a safe place because we don't have very many. Mom and Dad are going to bring more food when they come."

"When's that going to be?" Leila and Luke asked.

"I don't know. I just don't know. Hey, guys, let's see what we can do to straighten out everything and make it neater in here. Leila, why don't you get all of your things and put them on that ledge by where we slept last night. Luke, you can put all of your things here in this corner."

Adam moved his hand and felt around the corner. It was about six inches deep and three feet long and shaped like a triangular shelf. The ledge felt solid but had some loose rocks and dirt on top. Adam brushed the loose debris away for Luke, then walked to the back of the cave and rolled up their bedding as tight as he could. He stacked the jackets on top of the roll and pushed the pile against the cave wall.

Then, another aftershock hit, but this time it wasn't as strong. The feel of the ground moving under their feet was disorienting. It felt like they were falling even with their feet flat on the ground. All three of them stopped what they were doing until the trembling was over and rocks quit falling past the cave opening. They ran to the front of the cave and watched silently.

Adam was scared, but he couldn't let the kids see how worried he was. He could feel the tension in his muscles, and his stomach felt like it was in knots. Why hadn't their mom and dad returned by now? Maybe the earthquake had caused a road to close, forcing them to find a new route. He tried to estimate how much that might delay them and how soon they should get there. No matter which scenario he considered, he knew they should have been here long ago.

Suddenly, Adam had a feeling that their parents weren't coming back. All three of them were up here on the side of the mountain, in the middle of the Hoh National Forest, with no parents and no car.

"No car!" Adam yelled. His worry and fear began turning into anger. He had no car! They had no way of getting out of here! He felt confined. Adam started kicking the side of the cave entrance--knocking aside everything in his path. The rocks, however, stayed motionless, and by the third kick, Adam's ankle hurt. He kept on kicking and kicking repeatedly until the pain in his ankle overcame his anger. Realizing that his ankle hurt really bad, he finally quit. He hopped to the blankets on one foot. His foot hurt. Shaking, he just sat down right there.

When he glanced up toward the mouth of the cave, he saw Leila and Luke huddled together as if they were afraid of him, and he felt ashamed. He hadn't thought of them before he let his temper get out of hand. He hopped over to where they were, then bent his knees up under his chin and looked out of the cave and down the mountain. What were they going to do? He turned the question over and over in his mind. He quickly came up with, and discarded, several plans--many of which were completely unlikely. Finally, he had to accept that there was no quick solution to their problem. They had no choice but to wait.

"Kids, what do you say we just take us a little nap. That way, maybe it will seem like Mom and Dad will get here faster."

Luke sniffled and asked, "Will you tell us a story?"

"I'm just not in the mood for stories right now, Luke. Maybe tomorrow," Adam said. "I'll tell you what. Let's you, Leila, and I check out the food supply that Mom and Dad stored for us, and we'll get everything all neat for them."

Leila's face brightened, and her twelve-year-old psyche was immediately ready to move around and fix up the cave.

"Let's go!" she said as she prodded Luke. Adam realized that anything that reminded the kids of their parents' return restored their faith.

Adam, Leila, and Luke began putting their things in order. Adam decided to put all of his own personal items in the large trash can. That way, he knew that his own things would not be disturbed. He started with his clothes, then his iPod, his batteries, and his radio.

He spoke softly to himself, saying, "Why did I grab this radio anyway?"

That was when he remembered that Luke had bought it for him for Christmas and had been so proud because it had been his own idea. He had bought it by himself. Luke looked up to Adam, and that pleased Adam, even though Luke's whining was sometimes irritating. Sometimes when Luke watched Adam with those big, brown eyes trying, in his six-year-old way, to imitate him, Adam's ego got a real boost.

When they finished organizing their own things, they started looking through the food. They didn't find much.

"I'm hungry," Luke said.

Adam looked at his beans and macaroni and realized that they had no way to cook anything. And they had no canned food. The only food they could just eat was the same crackers and peanut butter they'd eaten before. Luke looked at Adam with disappointment in his eyes.

"Not again," he said.

"For now, I guess that is what we'll have to eat," Adam remembered his mom and dad and added, "until Mom and Dad get back."

They ate in silence, using Adam's pocket knife to spread the peanut butter. When they were finished, Adam noticed that it had gotten noticeably darker. Dusk had fallen. Again, Adam suggested that they bed down.

"Why don't we go to bed and sleep until Mom and Dad get back in the morning?"

Luke and Leila followed Adam back to the bed roll. They smoothed everything down the same way as the night before and got comfortable.

Again, the cave began shaking in the middle of the night. Again, another aftershock. The whole cave floor was moving as if they were laying on an air mattress in the water. They could hear more rocks falling down from higher up the mountain and could imagine more rocks falling across the cave entrance.

Leila was scared, but Luke remained asleep. "What was that?"

Then she screamed as the movement of the cave floor intensified.

"It was probably a small aftershock," Adam answered her, but in his mind he believed that it wasn't just an aftershock because the ground was shaking so much. Maybe it was even stronger than the first one.

He gave Leila a reassuring hug and said, "I'll be right back." Then, he climbed out from under the covers and worked his way toward the cave entrance to see if this one had closed them in. With his hands, he felt the wall as he went--checking for new cracks. He wondered if it would make it harder for his mom and dad to find them. A large earthquake hit last night too! Was that the reason their parents were not back, or were they detained by the guys trying to take over their house? Adam did not know.

He pushed back rocks that had fallen in front of the cave until he was tired, then he worked his way back to the kids. He pondered the logic of moving all three of them closer to the mouth of the cave, but Luke remained asleep, and the last thing he needed to deal with was Luke crying. His crying could be piercingly loud. Not only would it be annoying for him, but it would unnerve Leila as well. He gradually went back to sleep and tossed restlessly while wondering just what had really happened.

He stirred from his sleep when he noticed a small amount of light coming from the mouth of the cave. He looked at his watch, but couldn't yet read it. He went to the entrance but had to push more large rocks aside just to get out of the cave. He moved them carefully, trying to be quiet. He wanted the kids to stay asleep. After he walked around outside for a while, he went back into the cave. His doubts and fears had become so great, he felt the need for physical exertion.

He decided that he would go down the mountain on foot. He had no car and no way to get to town, or anywhere else, except on foot. His anger at his father's absence and stubbornness started to surface, but he realized that he had to quell the anger. He needed to help himself and the kids.

Leila and Luke began to stir. When they were fully awake, he told them, "I'm going to have to hike down the mountain to look for Mom and Dad. You guys can wait here for me."

"Adam! No! You can't leave us!" Luke said.

Leila yelled, "No! We will not stay here alone!"

Adam was irritated by their outburst. He reconsidered, though, when he looked at each of the two kids. They looked tired and scared. He couldn't be angry at them any more. "I guess we'll all have to go, then. But, first, we'll have to get ready. Let's eat first. "

"Please, not peanut butter again" both kids said.

Adam's worry and inability to get them out of this mess got the best of him. "Do you have a better idea? Go ahead. You can eat anything you please," he yelled.

He was worried, and his nerves were stretched to the limit. He felt cooped up and needed to get moving.

"I want a pop," Luke whispered very softly, while chewing on the ends of his fingers--an irritating and infantile habit.

"Like I said, get whatever you want. There might not be anything to eat all day."

"We're sorry," Leila answered.

"I'll tell you what, let's eat a little, and take some in our backpacks with us. We should all take our backpacks anyway. I'll take a couple of pops. You guys take a jar of peanut butter and a pack of crackers, and we'll eat them for lunch."

They silently sat eating a couple of crackers with peanut butter, and they finished one package of crackers.

"Leila, look here, we can use this package to wrap berries in if we find them."

The smile on Leila's face pleased and soothed Adam. They got ready and left to climb down the mountain. A short distance from the cave, the trail became very steep. Luke slipped on a piece of granite and fell. He screamed as he rolled several times before coming to a stop against a large, flat stone streaked with quartz. The bits of white were sharp. Adam slid down to Luke and gathered him into his arms.

"Okay, guys, let's do it this way. Follow me, single file, and we'll get down the mountain by walking a zigzag. Just be careful where you put your feet."

The kids made no comment, but they went silently down the mountain by following Adam until they reached the road. "Okay, now you guys can walk any way you want, but let's go as quickly as we can. We'll walk down the road, but if you hear someone coming, jump into the brush at the side and hide.

"Why?" Leila asked.

"It might be the guys who want our house."

Chapter 5 - The Forestry Cabin

They walked all morning, but they didn't see anyone, and they heard nothing. In a way, it was a relief to Adam. It also worried him. Why didn't their mom and dad come back? What caused them to disappear? Where was his car? What was going on with the invaders? All of these questions kept bouncing around in his mind, but he didn't dare voice his thoughts to the kids. He couldn't afford to scare them any more than they already were.

They came to a fork where a dirt road turned off the paved route. "Let's take the dirt road," Adam said. He was curious about the road. He didn't remember seeing it before, but he knew there were some ranger stations in the area. He also knew there were some Forest Service cabins nearby. If the road led to a cabin, and someone was there, maybe he could get some information. It would be worth it to spend the time finding out what was going on.

They walked until the sun was almost overhead, but they saw nothing. Luke became tired, and they decided to sit down and rest. Adam got out the crackers that Leila had packed. They ate the crackers and peanut butter until the crackers were gone, then drank a can of pop. It was warm, but refreshingly wet. It satisfied them.

Luke wanted another pop, but Adam said, "We'll need it for the trip back. We can't afford to drink it all at once."

"But I thought we were going to find Mom and Dad," Luke said.

"If we don't, then we have no choice but to walk all the way back to the cave. We don't want to see anyone except Mom and Dad right now. What if we were taken hostage by the men who want money for our house? What would we do then? We know that they are probably looking for us."

Leila asked Adam, "Do you have any money? You could just pay them the money, and then we could go home."

"The last time I tried to get money from my debit card, it wouldn't let me. I don't know everything that is going on."

He got up. "Let's go. It is getting late."

They continued down the dirt road. The road was covered with grass, except for ruts from a car or truck that had been using the road. The grass in the middle of the road was bent; the tallest blades were broken. Adam guessed that a vehicle had been down the road since the last rain had occurred the week before.

There had been no deer, squirrels, or other wildlife except a few small birds in the trees. Adam was used to seeing all kinds of wildlife and deer all over the place.

Finally, he saw what he thought was a roof. He quickened his pace and felt his heart race. He hurried down the trail until he saw a cabin that looked like a ranger station.

"Stay here, and just sit down a bit," he told the kids. If you hear anything, then run to the bushes and stay quiet."

"I'm scared," Leila said, but she sat down with her arm around Luke.

Adam stepped onto the porch and tried the front door. It was locked. He peeked into the small, four-pane window but saw no one inside. He saw that the front room was a combined kitchen and living room. A doorway in the middle of the room opened into what appeared to be a small hallway. He walked around the house and decided that there were two bedrooms and a bathroom at the rear of the cabin.

He heard a crash and turned away from the house. Through the brush, he saw a brown torrent of water. Another crash rang through the woods. Adam saw part of the bank fall. The air smelled of damp earth. Water was rising. He ran to the front of the house and grabbed a piece of kindling from a woodpile near the door. He smacked it into the front window, and a piece of glass fell to the wood below, making a *clinking* sound. He hit another pane, and more pieces fell. The sound of rushing water increased.

Suddenly, from what would have been the backyard of the house, a tree groaned as it fell into the rising water. They had to get out of there! Adam grabbed a large block of wood from the pile and threw it, aiming for the middle of the wood slats which supported the panes of glass. The wood broke, and most of the glass fell to the ground. The next time, he hit the glass even harder until he had most of the glass broken out. Grabbing a larger piece of wood, he slammed it against the wood supports, but they were much more difficult to break in. He put all of his strength into the cross pieces, and the bottom of the little window broke out. Then, using kindling along the edge of the window, he pushed in the rest of the glass and wood until it was clear.

He jumped into the house through the window, ran to the door and unlocked it, shoving it open as hard as he could. "You kids stay put," he said to Luke and Leila.

"What if you get in trouble?" Leila yelled at him.

"It wouldn't be the first time," he yelled to Luke and Leila.

Running back into the house, he threw open each cabinet--all of them. In one cabinet, he found a box of large trash bags. He pulled one out, then threw the remainder of the box into the sack. He started grabbing things. There was a tea kettle on the stove that he grabbed and threw into the sack. He found an old coffee cup with a screw-on cap. He rinsed it out, filled it with water, put the lid back on tight, and tossed it into his sack. He grabbed all the canned food from the cabinet. He also found some more crackers and some packages of dried meat. He threw these into the sack along with a container of oatmeal.

He opened the oven and found a dirty skillet which he tossed into the sack. Then, he opened the refrigerator and found some beer and pop. There were also two dozen eggs and a block of cheese. After putting these into his sack, he realized it was full. He took out the skillet and set it back on top of the stove, filling it with two smaller pans, a plastic bowl, some plastic dishes, and a small box of disposable knives and forks from another cabinet. He grabbed the skillet and, dragging the sack behind him, ran out the door. Another tree crashed into the rising water. Adam handed the heavy skillet to Leila and yelled, "Run up the road."

They ran until they heard a loud crash. Adam looked behind them and saw the roof of the cabin tilt away from him. Luke and Leila wanted to go back and look at the water.

Adam said, "We don't know how far up the water will go. We have to keep going. We've got to get out of here before something else

41

goes wrong." He was behind them, urging them on.

Leila and Luke asked in unison, "What's wrong, Adam?"

"I don't know. I don't know for sure, but I do know that we have been having earthquakes. The rising water might have something to do with the earthquakes. Maybe it is a tsunami. It's late; we need to get as far as we can before dark. Then we need to find a hiding place."

He looked down at his bulky trash sack and noticed that sharp objects had punched several holes in the sack. He had to make some adjustments.

"Hand me that skillet," he said to Leila.

The skillet wouldn't fit into any of their backpacks. He put the crackers and plastic utensils into Luke's bag. He put some of the canned food and the jerky packages into Leila's pack. He got out another large trash bag, put what was left inside, and balanced this bag over his shoulder.

"Let's get out of here as fast as we can," he repeated.

The three walked silently until Leila began complaining about the weight of the skillet. Luke carried it for a while. They got back to the main road and headed toward the cave. Dusk was coming on fast for a late October day, but they continued on up the road for a while.

As they rounded the curve in the road, they heard the high-pitched whine of an airplane engine coming toward them. Adam pulled the younger kids off the road. They ducked behind trees and crouched close to the ground. They looked down the road and didn't see anything, but the noise grew louder. A medium-sized plane, with water-landing gear, was flying almost overhead. The engine noise became a roar as the plane came closer. The sound slowly decreased and faded as it skimmed the treetops and faded into the background noise of the forest.

The kids remained frozen to the ground. They stayed hidden for a while after the sound of the plane had disappeared. It wasn't until a stellar jay bird flew over them and screeched that the kids began moving a little. Adam found himself shaking. The day had been just too much. "Let's just walk a little farther, then we'll stop and get a bite to eat."

"But I'm hungry now!" wailed Luke.

Adam's patience with everything had ended. It had been too much.

He yelled at Luke, "All you do is whine. Why don't you just shut up?"

Adam kicked the bush he'd just been hiding behind--kicked it over and over until his leg ached. His anger spent, he fell to the ground.

"We don't have any more peanut butter and crackers, but we do have some plain crackers. And we have more pop and a little water. And, I forgot, we now have some packaged jerky."

Leila spoke almost in a whisper, "Could we have one of those packages of jerky?"

She pulled the package out of her backpack.

"But I don't like jerky," Luke whined. "And all you do is yell at me, and I want Mom and Dad!"

Adam simply replied, "Fine, don't eat any."

Then he opened up a beer and handed Leila a pop. Sipping the liquid seemed to calm them down some.

Luke whispered, "Can I have some pop and crackers?"

Wordlessly, Adam handed him some crackers and a pop. He could tell that he wasn't cut out to be taking care of kids. However, at this time, he had no choice until their parents returned. He thought to himself, *Where are Mom and Dad?* Out loud, he said, "Let's go."

Adam and the two kids got up, not even bothering to brush the leaves and pine needles off their clothes. Adam felt itchy, and he needed a shower. He was tired of having to look after the kids, and he just wanted to be alone.

"I didn't want you guys to come along anyway," he said to the two kids--but softly, so that they didn't hear him.

None of this was Adam's choice, and it made him so mad that he had to deal with it. His foot hurt where he had kicked the bush so many times. Silently, they walked down the road. Adam walked in the middle of the road while Luke and Leila trailed behind, holding hands. He had never been very close to the two, mostly because they had each other and didn't need him. No one ever needed Adam, and maybe that was why he got angry so easily. But now that the kids needed him, he still got angry, and they just got closer to each other. In his mind, Adam had never felt more alone.

Dusk was creeping into the woods, and the sounds were changing. Even though Adam had been camping many times in the woods, noises in the dark spooked him. Birds were quiet, and he could hear the sound of his shoes hitting the road each time he stepped on the black of the asphalt. He realized that they couldn't make it back to the cave before nightfall. How could he solve this problem?

He was still chewing on the jerky, and it tasted good. The mountain air became cooler and cooler. Every now and then he heard a branch snap or the tops of the trees rustle. There was a bit of mist in the air, and he hoped it wouldn't rain, but he knew it was a possibility. Adam smelled the musky scent of moist air that occurs just before a rain.

Adam heard Luke whisper to Leila, "I'm getting cold and tired."

Darkness came quickly, and the outlines of the trees began to fade. It would soon be too dark to see. Adam saw a little group of Douglas fir trees that were grouped together in a small clearing.

"I guess we'll spend the night here," he said. "We have no blankets. I didn't think we'd be stuck out here without any place to keep warm. We have matches at the cave, but not here, and we don't have much to eat unless I open a can of food."

"But we don't have a can opener." Leila told him.

Adam hadn't thought about a can opener. They didn't have one here or in the cave, but he still had his pocket knife. The cave seemed so far away. It had become their own safe place, and he would have loved to be in that cave right now--even without a shower.

He reached into the sack and pulled out a can. He couldn't quite read what was in it, but he knew it would be something they could eat. He pulled out his pocket knife and sat down to open the can. He used the knife to cut into the can just below the rim, and he worked it all the way around. Both kids were peering toward Adam, watching him work. Finally, he pushed up the top of the can and created an opening over about half of the can. The edges were very rough and sharp. The contents smelled pungent and spicy. He stuck in his finger, tasted it, and said, "It's chili!"

Luke forgot about Adam's anger and said, "Wow! How did you do that?"

Adam said nothing, but he smiled at Luke. He reached his hand down into the sack he'd carried from the cabin and felt around until he found the package of plastic eating utensils and pulled out a spoon. He stuck it into the top of the can. The lid was still attached, with the edges rough and sharp. The top content of the can was thick, so he stirred together the juice, fat, and beans with meat. Even cold, it tasted good.

"Guys, it even tastes like chili!" he said. "Here, Luke, just eat a few spoons of the chili, then let Leila have some, and I'll eat what is left. Be careful, though, and don't let your hands touch the top of the can because it will cut you. Be sure you don't spill any because I don't know if we even have anymore. I don't know what is in the sack. I just grabbed what I could, as fast as I could, at that cabin."

Adam sipped the beer while, one at a time, the kids ate. Then they shared a pop while Adam ate the remainder of the chili. They were beginning to get used to sharing.

As he drank the beer, for the first time Adam noticed a chill in the air. They were going to have to find a way to stay warm and avoid hypothermia. He'd get them more comfortable, but it wouldn't be easy. Not with the kids. Again, he wished all of them were back at the cave. It would be even better if their mom and dad would return. The seat of his pants felt damp, and Adam realized that fog would probably be setting in because the air was so wet, it was almost dripping. Everything smelled damp. He put his hand down onto the leaves. They were wet. The dampness and darkness made the grove of trees seem even more eerie. Adam sipped the last of his beer and idly began digging around in the large garbage sack. He was lucky that the box of trash bags were the large, heavy ones. He pulled out the small, folded Army surplus shovel and turned it over in his hands. He could barely remember grabbing the small shovel, folding down the handle, and tossing it into the sack just as he went out the door.

An idea formed in his mind. Adam finished his beer and removed four trash bags from the pack. He had a plan, and he hoped it would work.

Chapter 6 - Night in the woods

Adam glanced at Leila and Luke and noticed they were already huddled together with Leila holding Luke as if she were protecting him. He couldn't see their faces very well, but they looked scared. Adam had calmed down, but he was scared himself. *And after all, they are even younger than me*, he thought. He knew he would have to keep a lid on his temper. He just wasn't sure how to do that. He didn't want the job of taking care of two kids, but he had it anyway. Until his parents returned, he knew that he had to rely on himself. Adam had always considered himself to be a very independent person, but he was finding out just how much he relied on his parents.

He picked up one of the trash sacks and folded it down the middle. Using his pocket knife, he cut a triangle out of the middle-- about five inches down from the top. He picked up the other two bags and did the same thing. Then he spoke softly to the kids. "Leila and Luke, come here a second."

"What are you going to do?" Leila asked.

"Just come here and watch," he told them. He opened one of the trash bags and slipped it over Luke's head. It covered him almost to his ankles. Then he got the other one and, after a small adjustment to the hole, slipped it over Leila's head. The trash bag covered Leila almost to her knees. "Now you both have a raincoat."

Luke whispered, "But I can't use my arms."

"Hmm. You can't, but we're going to have to sleep here. If there are no more holes, it might keep you warmer." Adam was careful to keep his voice low. He felt that he was at least finally understanding more about not letting their circumstances get to him.

"I think it's cool," Leila said. "How did you think of this?"

"I'm just trying to take care of us," he told her.

"You guys just sit tight, and I'll be over there for a while, okay?" Even though it was almost dark, Adam pointed to a small grove of trees.

He took another sack and walked out from under the fir trees. His footsteps sounded twice as loud in the silence of the woods at night than they did in the daylight. Soon he felt the ground change into a quieter softness. He opened the shovel and the sack and began shoveling the pine needles, leaves, and forest floor duff into the sack until it was filled. He then returned to the kids.

"Okay, Luke, go pee behind that tree, and come right back."

Luke left. Adam told Leila to do the same, but in the opposite direction. He kneeled down next to a small clump of trees and waited until the kids got back.

"You guys," he said, "lie down here--against this tall tree."

They did, and Adam stood up and grabbed his sack of forest duff and debris. He knelt down by Luke and poured the leaves over him. "Stay there," he said. Then he repeated the process and poured the forest floor bedding over Leila.

"But how will you stay warm?" Luke thoughtfully asked.

Adam got a sack and filled it. He picked up another sack, enlarged the hole, and put it over his head. It fit. He grabbed the filled sack and dumped it over his legs, then settled down next to Leila and Luke. He realized that staying together kept them warmer. He fell asleep listening to a small breeze that caused the branches overhead to make a very soft rustling sound.

All three slept until light began to burn through the fog. Adam woke up and watched as the light gradually increased, driving the fog away. The smell of damp forest duff and cedar surrounded them. Adam liked the smell of the forest. Leila, only slightly awake, snuggled closer to Adam. It warmed him from the inside, and he liked the feel of being so close to someone. It was an entirely new experience for him. He found himself feeling emotionally close to his sister, and he'd never even allowed himself to be close to his own mother. Opening up to his father was unthinkable. Thinking of his dad ruined the mood for Adam.

"Guys, let's get up so we can get back to the cave."

They pushed aside the leaves and pulled off their sacks. Carefully,

Adam folded the sacks and handed them back to Luke and Leila. They put them in their backpacks.

"Let's go. Maybe we can wait to eat until we get back, but I don't know how far away we are. It's uphill all the way, and we are carrying things now."

"Do I have to carry that old, dirty skillet? It has some grease in it, and it is heavy and yucky." Leila held the skillet as if it weighed fifty pounds.

Adam remembered the feeling of affection he'd had earlier, so he said, "I'll tell you what. I'll try to get it into the big sack and carry it until it gets too heavy. Will you carry the shovel?" He wanted her to see that they had to work together.

Luke asked Adam, "Could we have some jerky to chew on while we walk?

"You bet!"

As an afterthought, Adam reached into the sack, got out a pop, opened it, and handed it to Luke. The drink was passed around until it was finished. Adam got himself a piece of jerky to chew on and offered Luke and Leila a piece. They each had something to chew on, so they started walking. He slung the large trash bag over his shoulder, and he thought of the images of children running away from home with their belongings. He remembered his favorite story of *Oliver Twist*, and how he'd had to run. Adam wondered what the kids were thinking, but he remained silent and tried to keep his mind alert.

Finally, the daylight moved the fog up higher and visibility was better. Adam glanced back behind them. While the actual slope wasn't great, they had walked downhill most of the day before. This time, they had to climb while carrying their new supplies. He wished they were back at the cave because he was still tired. Although he had slept okay the night before, the stress of the previous few days had been exhausting. It seemed the sack got heavier with each step. Adam concentrated on just placing one foot in front of the other. He shifted the heavy sack several times but finally had to sit down right in the middle of the road. He wasn't afraid someone would come along anymore. He wondered if the earthquakes had caused a road to collapse like the Nisqually earthquake had done to Highway 101.

Adam opened another pop and took the first drink this time. "Leila, you've got to carry the skillet for a while. We do really need it;

I don't want to leave it behind. Try putting it on your head like Johnny Appleseed, and just use one hand at a time to keep it up there."

"Do I have to put that dirty thing on top of my head?"

"You do unless you can think of a better way." He pulled the skillet out of the sack and handed it to Leila but didn't say anything else.

She handed the shovel back to Adam, but Luke grabbed it. "I can carry it," Luke said. This surprised Adam.

They started walking up the long road. They were tired, hot, and hungrier than ever. Their pace had slowed, and Adam noticed that Leila had shifted the skillet onto her head. She was also taking Adam's advice to alternate hands while holding it there. She held the skillet upright on her head, which would make it harder, but Adam didn't say anything. They trudged on.

Adam looked ahead and noticed that the road looked like a part in a man's hair. In his fatigue, he began to imagine the trees moving, but he began to recognize the moss pattern on the trees. He also recognized the trees close to the road. It began to sprinkle lightly, but they walked on. Finally, Leila said, "I just can't carry this skillet anymore."

They stopped walking. Adam stood there wondering what he could do. He noticed a clump of bushes to the right of the road. He took the skillet from Leila and put it behind the bushes, being careful to hide it well. Then, he gathered a pile of sticks and tree cones, put the pile next to the road, got a stick, and pushed it into the ground until only about six inches were sticking out.

Forcing a smile, he turned to the kids and said, "Let's get going. Who knows? Maybe Mom and Dad are looking for us around the cave."

He didn't really think so, but he had to keep the kids walking. All three of them needed food and rest--and their parents. Adam never thought he'd see the day when he wished for both of his parents. If for nothing else, to take care of the kids. He liked it better when he only had to worry about himself. Maybe that was why he never had a serious girlfriend. The minute a girl acted like she liked him, he was ready to find another friend. He didn't really want to take care of someone else. Somehow Adam was coming to realize this.

They trudged on--hot, tired, and hungry--but they also began noticing more landmarks that they recognized. Each time Adam recognized a tree, a patch of open meadow, or a clump of bushes, he walked faster. He noticed the tire tracks where his dad's car had turned off the road into a small meadow to park. Luke and Leila also noticed and started running toward the cave. Adam just kept trudging along, trying to keep moving in spite of the heavy sack.

Then, there it was. The cave. Adam couldn't wait to get back inside. He would be so glad to dump that load. The place that he'd been so against moving to now seemed like a haven. It was far better than being out on the road with the kids. Then he remembered that the skillet was still hidden beside the road. He still had to go back to get the skillet.

He entered the cave and put down the sack. He went to the bedroll and leaned against it. Both kids followed his example.

"Adam," Luke said, "Mom and Dad still aren't here."

"You are right."

"What should we do? We didn't find them in two days of looking for them."

Adam stretched out his tall, thin frame and tried to think about their problems. Before he could come up with any solution, he realized it was already afternoon, and he was hungry. He remembered the small pan inside the sack. He told Luke and Leila to go outside and collect some small, dry twigs for a fire. Then he dug around in the large trash can and found one of the packages of macaroni. They had no milk or salt, but they now had some cheese and more jerky. He got a piece of jerky and broke open the packages of cheese and macaroni. He went to the sack he'd just dumped onto the cave floor and dug out the small pan. Then he went to the mouth of the cave, where water was always dripping, and filled the pan half-full of water.

Luke and Leila brought in some small brush, and Luke and Adam broke it into small pieces. They placed it in the back of the cave and tried to use a match to start a fire, but the wood was too wet to burn. The fire didn't start.

"Go get some leaves--as dry as you can find--and some very tiny twigs," he told the kids.

They kept working, but by the time they got the fire going, they had used several matches. Realizing that they didn't have many matches left, Adam wondered how he could improvise a way to save coals like they did in ancient days. When some coals had built up, and they had used up all the sticks, Luke and Leila got more twigs from outside. Adam put them on the fire one at a time to keep it small. Then he put the pan directly onto the little fire, watching as the water heated. He put the pieces of jerky into the pan, and when the water boiled, he added some macaroni. Adam's mouth was already watering as he anticipated eating a hot meal--even though it was just macaroni.

"Luke, where is your backpack?" he asked. "Bring it here."

Luke brought the backpack to him, and Adam removed the plastic plates, forks, and spoons. "Guys, we're going to have to hang onto these, so we'll wipe them off and use them again. Don't break them if you can help it."

Finally, the macaroni seemed soft enough to eat, so he added some chunks of cheese. He split the food three ways. It didn't taste like home-cooked macaroni, but it was good. Adam watched the reaction of the kids to his meal. Luke looked at Adam as if he was going to say something, but he didn't. He ate while making a face, and Leila did the same thing.

"You don't cook like Mom," Leila said, but she and Luke went on eating.

When the macaroni was finished, they split a pop. Adam mentally surveyed how many pops they had left. He thought the number was four, but he'd check later. For now, he had to get that skillet. "Guys, I'm going to have to go back after that skillet," he told them. "And, no, you aren't going because it isn't far, and I'll be right back. You guys get some more sticks and wood while it is still daylight. Try to keep the fire going, but keep it small."

Adam had just enough daylight left to get there, so he left quickly. He entered back into the light outside. He went down the side of the mountain to the road, then continued downhill, looking for the marker he had left.

Chapter 7 - Water

As Adam walked, he felt suddenly free, like a weight had been lifted off his shoulders. No kids.

He was not cut out for watching kids. Maybe he shouldn't even have any of his own if it was always this difficult. He followed the road, watching for his pile of sticks used to mark where he left the skillet. Watching the road carefully, he let his eyes wander into the brush. He saw a small road that he had not noticed before. It angled up the mountain. Curious, Adam turned onto the dirt road. The ruts were overgrown with grass, making it look like it hadn't been used in years. It looked like an old logging road. He followed the road for a short distance, and then he heard the gurgling sound of a rushing stream. Soon, he could smell the fresh scent of the stream. The musty scent of dampness drew him closer to the fresh water, a scent he'd always liked.

Enjoying the freedom of not having to think about the kids, Adam picked up his speed and walked up to a small creek. He sat down, pulled off the socks on his tired feet, pulled up his pants legs, and walked into the water. The creek came halfway up the calves of his legs. He bent over and washed his face and hair.

"Geez, this feels good," he said out loud.

He walked down the little stream and found a place where the bottom was more sandy than rocky. Then, he picked up a stick and pushed aside some of the sand and rocks, making the stream a little deeper. He tossed the stick aside and used both hands to clear out a deeper hole in the creek bottom. He couldn't help thinking about the kids. He stood in the middle of the stream and listened to the trickling bubble of the stream water as it moved over the stream bed. He picked up a small pebble and dropped it into the water just to see what it would do. It made a *kerplink* sound as it disappeared. In seconds, the water was as if there had never been an outside intrusion. Just water. He stooped over and gathered water into both his hands and let it trickle through his fingers.

The feeling rejuvenated Adam. Overcome by an impulse, he climbed out of the water and pulled off all of his clothes, then returned to the stream. The cold water hit him like a slap on the face, but when he hunkered down into the water where the air couldn't hit him, it didn't seem so cold. He tried washing but had nothing to use for a cloth, so he jumped out of the water and grabbed his underwear. As fast as he could, he returned to the stream and, making sure he kept under the water, he used the underwear to wash himself. He had to remain prone to keep water on top of him, and it was awkward because his butt kept hitting the sand. The sand felt funny, but the water did feel good. So good.

Adam noticed that the sun was beginning to recede, so he jumped back out and shook the water from his hair. He pushed his hands down his legs, stripping off the water. He shook off more water and pulled on his pants. He left his wet underwear on a rock like a discarded dishrag. When he got the rest of his clothes on, he felt warmer. He looked at his wet underwear, picked them up, and wrung out as much of the water as he could.

He picked up his stick, pushed one end in a loop in back of his pants, looped the wet underwear on the stick, then stuck the other end of the stick into the other back loop.

"I'll bring the kids here tomorrow and we'll wash up," he said to himself. The trees rustled slightly at the very tops, and he heard the sounds of a few birds. Bird sounds always made him feel more secure in the woods. To warm up, he ran down the old road, passing the brush which crowded both sides. At some places, the road was so overgrown that Adam skipped sideways to avoid branches. He ran to the end of the small road and continued down the larger paved route. It didn't take him long to find the skillet and pick it up. He was beginning to warm up. He decided to keep running. It felt good. He didn't have to slow his pace for the kids.

This feels wonderful, he thought. It didn't take long for the skillet to get heavy, and Adam began shifting it from one arm to the other. He finally turned it upside down and carried it the rest of the way on his head--Johnny Appleseed style. He couldn't run this way, but he could walk fast. Dark was catching up with him, so he watched very carefully for the place to turn and climb toward the cave.

Adam continued farther than he remembered. He began to fear that he'd missed the trail for the turnoff to the cave, and he was getting very nervous. The birds had become quiet, and the fog was starting to set in again, making it increasingly difficult to see. Just as he was about to turn around, Adam passed a small clearing and found the familiar turnaround where his dad had parked their car. Relieved, he headed toward the cave.

It was a big relief to get into the cave, and Adam found himself happy to see the kids. Sure enough, they had gathered a large pile of sticks and had kept the small fire going.

"Adam, you look silly with your underwear hanging on that stick, and your underwear looks wet." Leila said.

"I found some water. I'll take you there tomorrow. Washing up feels so good."

"What kind of water? Did you find a house?"

"No, it is a very small creek, but it is big enough for us to wash. I already tried it, and it was cold, but I felt better after I got on my dry clothes."

"I'm not washing in cold water," Leila said.

"We'll see."

Tentatively, Luke said to Adam, "We drank a pop." He backed away and watched for Adam's response.

Adam was about to say something curt until he noticed how Luke was backing away from him. He also saw Luke's watery eyes. He appeared to be on the verge of tears. Instead, he said, "Guess that's okay, Luke, but you do need to realize that when the pop is gone, we might not be able to find more."

Leila stepped up to defend Luke, "We'd been gathering wood, and we were both thirsty. We are hungry, too, and your macaroni wasn't all that good." She relaxed like she'd gotten it all out. Adam noticed that both of the kids seemed afraid of him. Here he was trying to help them, and they were afraid of him. Just thinking about it was irritating, but he was too tired to react.

Adam got an idea. "Let's see what we can find out about Mom

54

and Dad," he told the kids.

Leila asked, "How are we going to do that?"

"I have a radio, remember? And, I have batteries for it. Let's get it out before it gets completely dark."

Adam went to his large trash can and tipped it over so that he could retrieve the radio. He had to crawl part of the way into the plastic trash can to get the batteries. He set the can upright and sat down to put the batteries into the radio. When he turned the radio on, every station was in Spanish. They didn't understand a thing that was being broadcast. The kids looked up at Adam, then looked back at the radio as if it were a snake. The announcements concluded, then music started--also in Spanish. The music was lively and bright, but the kids didn't understand the words. The three of them just sat frozen while they listened to the radio broadcast in Spanish.

He kept hearing the word "*suelo*."

"Let's just leave the radio on for a bit while I find us something to eat." Just the sound of the radio seemed to make the dire cave a little less lonely.

"I stacked the food from your sack here. I hope it's okay with you."

Adam glanced toward the edge of the cave wall and noticed that Leila had stacked the cans by type. There were several cans of chili, soup, and peaches. Adam's mouth watered at the thought of the peaches. Then he noticed that she had stacked the pop next to the beer. He had three cans left, and he was going to have one this evening before he went to bed. He got the coffee cup that was full of water and drank half of it, then looked at Luke and Leila.

"Do you want some water?" he handed the cup to Leila. The two kids finished off the cup of water. "Let's have peaches for supper." Adam noticed that there were six cans and decided that they'd eat two of them. He could save the cans to use as makeshift soup bowls. They had to utilize what they had.

"Leila, get me two of those cans of peaches. Luke, get us three spoons from our plastic tableware."

Adam took his pocket knife out and opened it to the small blade. When Leila handed him a can, he began carefully opening it, but juice leaked out and spilled all over. He set down the can of peaches and cut the top off an empty beer can. Then he held the topless beer can under the slit in the can of peaches and drained out the juice until no more ran out. He finished cutting off the top of the can of peaches, poured the juice back into the can, and handed it to Luke.

"Eat only about half of the can," Adam told him. While Luke was eating, Adam did the same thing with the other can of peaches and gave it to Leila.

"Only half," he said. As Leila and Luke were eating, the radio suddenly changed languages. Both children stopped eating, with spoons in mid-air. Adam found himself holding his breath.

"There will be only two weeks left of this daily broadcast in English. The Democratic Latin Alliance will fine anyone caught speaking English after that time. It is suggested by the government that you learn Spanish as quickly as possible.

"Now, about the earthquake. The north tip of the Olympic Peninsula has been cut off by water. Mount Rainier is rumbling and showing signs of erupting. Sea planes have been sent to the new island, which has been named *El Cuarto*, and all survivors have been picked up. There will be more patrols flying *El Cuarto* to make sure that no one has been left. Most of the people aren't descendants of Latin nations, so they were homeless anyway. Work camps have been set up for those who refuse to pay rent to the Democratic Latin Alliance, or people who are not of Latin descent."

Adam and the two children were frozen in place staring at the radio. The big question: "Where are Mom and Dad?" entered the minds of all three.

Adam was thinking, *I could survive so much easier by myself.*

As if Leila could read Adam's mind, she wrapped Luke in her protective arms and asked, "Adam, you'll help us, won't you?"

It seemed to Adam that Luke and Leila had each other--leaving him alone. Like it had always been. Yet, Adam knew that he couldn't abandon his own brother and sister. He would have to find a way to get the three of them to think and act like a team--like it was at work. He turned his attention back to the radio.

"Seattle and Bremerton are completely under water. Some people have been rescued, but casualties have been high. Many towns along the Hood Canal are not there anymore. Those people who looked like Latin citizens were picked up by rescue boats, but there weren't enough boats to pick up everyone. The Latin citizens come first.

"This concludes the broadcast for today. The Democratic Latin Alliance station will provide news in English for thirteen more days. The broadcast will be at this same time each day for one hour only."

The two children glanced at each other. They looked at Adam for reassurance. "Do you think Mom and Dad are okay?" they asked.

"Let's think about what we can do right now--like eating."

Leila and Luke finished eating their partial cans of peaches. They each handed their cans to Adam, who got each one to eat a little more. "Drink the juice, too, because there is nutrition in the juice."

"I don't like the juice," whined Luke.

"Then don't drink it, but don't throw it away either," Adam said. "I'm certainly not going to make you eat" He felt his anger prickling, and he added, "But you both have to realize that Mom and Dad are not going to be able to get back very soon, and we have very little food. What's more, the food we have won't be like what we had at home. Our macaroni was probably good compared to what we'll be able to eat from now on. If we don't get some food, we'll die. It's that simple. Why don't you drink only water tonight, and you can have one pop a day until they are all gone? I'll drink water or beer. I'll let you two decide when you drink your pop and how. How about that?"

Luke and Leila began quarreling over when they would drink their pop. Luke wanted to do it at bedtime, but Leila wanted early afternoon. Leila didn't want to get up in the cold and go to the bathroom.

Adam banked dirt around the coals of the fire, and tried to fix it so that some of the coals would last all night. "Let's get some sleep, and we'll think about this tomorrow. Mom and Dad can't get to us, so we'll probably have to wait until we get rid of the Democratic Latin Alliance."

Luke asked him, "How will that happen?"

"I don't know. I just know it is our only hope for freedom."

Leila asked, "Wouldn't it be better to be caught so that we can be with Mom and Dad?"

"We might have to, but do you want to be in a work camp where you work, but don't get paid? Besides that, what makes you think that the Democratic Latin Alliance will bother finding our parents for us? Remember that they were kicking us out of our house." Neither of the kids answered Adam. They sat down silently, looking to Adam for answers.

After a couple of minutes of silence, Adam said, "Let's get ready for bed."

They put on their sweats and crawled onto the bedding. Adam ate the peaches and opened one can of beer. He walked to the opening of the cave and looked out, trying to figure how the three of them were going to survive. It would not be easy.

"You guys be sure to go to the bathroom before you go to bed because then you won't have to get up. I'm not very good at being Mom and Dad, so you are going to have to learn to do your own thinking, and try whining and complaining a little less."

As he looked outside, Adam realized that he felt comfortable inside the cave. At least they were dry and hidden. Softly, to himself, he said, "I don't think Mom and Dad have survived that earthquake."

For a second, Adam considered giving up to the authorities. Deep inside, though, he knew that he didn't want to be a captive. Something inside him made him resist being held in a work camp. The feeling of resistance grew stronger in him. He'd begun to think of himself as a resistor to what had happened to his country.

He did consider the possibility of letting the kids stand in an open area when they heard a plane and letting them get caught while he hid. That way, he would have only himself to worry about. He watched Leila coming back to the cave and realized that the kids would not be able to resist questioning about Adam. He sipped his beer slowly, knowing that it would soon be gone.

Carefully, the children slipped behind Adam at the mouth of the cave--scraping against the wall rather than allowing themselves to get any closer to him than necessary.

He continued sipping his beer and thinking he'd find a way to survive. He'd never be a part of the Democratic Latin Alliance. NEVER! NEVER! Thinking this way built up tension within Adam until he remembered that their dad has been a bad drinker and cussed and swore when he drank beer. Adam vowed to be different. Maybe the kids were remembering their dad and not thinking about Adam. He realized that now he was the only dad the kids had. Thinking this way made him feel more protective toward them. He went outside the cave, wandering around for a while to unwind, then slowly reentered. He tossed the empty can in the pile by the wall. He noticed that Leila really had organized things inside the cave, and he was thankful for her efforts.

When he crawled on the pallet they had fixed for themselves, he found himself next to Luke.

Softly, Luke told Adam, "I'm scared about Mom and Dad."

Adam turned on his side, putting one arm around Luke. "It's okay, Luke, we'll just have to help each other. Can I have you make sure the fire is always ready with wood and leaves for burning? It looks like Leila has appointed herself the official cavekeeper. And I'll be the CEO of the island of *El Quarto*. Tomorrow, we'll go to the creek and wash."

Chapter 8 - The Stream

Adam had to get up during the night, and he stood outside the cave looking down the slope of the mountain. The quiet was almost complete except for light movement of leaves in the tops of the trees. No birds sang. Each of his footsteps made a soft *thud-squish-thud* as he walked, and Adam decided he sort of liked the absence of urban sounds. Urban sounds were harsh, while the sound of natural life in the woods was a soft sound. He liked listening to the quiet. He looked toward the sky but couldn't see anything. Stars weren't visible, so he could see only a few feet in front of himself. He went back inside the cave to the pallet and snuggled tight against Luke. It made him feel a little closer to him. He slept until daylight started peeking through the crack in the rock that formed the cave opening.

Adam's mouth felt and tasted horrible, so he got a twig, peeled off the bark with his knife, and used it as a toothpick to clean his teeth. It felt a lot better, but his mouth still tasted terrible. He dug around in the food and found an open jar of peanut butter. He spooned out some peanut butter and ate it plain. Seeing the eggs gave him the idea to cook some for breakfast--even though there wasn't any fat to cook them in.

After walking to the fire area, he uncovered the dirt. The spot was still warm, but the coals were completely gone. He'd have to figure out a way to keep coals going through the night. He dug out some of the leaves and twigs that Luke and Leila had gathered the day before and carefully piled them together. He struck a match, but it wouldn't light. He got the small fire started with the second match. Having dry material and a warm fire area helped him get the fire started easier. He did a mental count of the matches that were left, and realized that he'd have to be careful about using them.

It sure was nice to have a little fire in the cave. There weren't any rocks around the cave, but he could get some really good ones when they went to the stream. He prepared to cook the eggs.

Luke and Leila woke up, and Luke went outside.

"Adam, what are you doing?" Leila asked.

"I'm going to cook us some eggs," Adam answered her.

"You can't use that skillet. It's dirty."

"I'm going to burn off the dirt with the fire. Eggs don't need much fire to cook, but we'll have to scramble them."

"We don't have any bacon or sausage. And we don't have any toast."

Adam was getting irritated again but didn't say anything. He was hungry and eager to get back to the little creek. He simply continued heating the skillet and turned it upside down to get the burned grease out. He set the hot skillet down and broke six eggs into it. Adam's mouth started watering, but then he realized that the eggs would have very little flavor. Without salt, they weren't going to be good. He looked around and noticed the cans of chili. He opened one of the cans and put about a fourth of the contents into the eggs, then returned the whole thing to the little fire. He had only a stick to stir with, and the eggs began sticking to the skillet, so he stirred even harder to keep the eggs from burning on the bottom. He added some chunks of the cheese. When he finished, he got three plates, and divided the food into three equal portions. He couldn't get the stuck part of the eggs off the bottom, so he put some water into the skillet and set it aside to take care of later.

Leila had gone outside, and Luke was back. "Is that our breakfast? I'm hungrier than that!"

"We are just going to have to get used to eating less because we don't know how long it will take Mom and Dad to find us."

Leila, back from outside, got three forks and gave one to each of them.

"Make sure you save these," Adam said.

When they had finished eating, the kids went to the back of the cave and started pulling off the sweats they had slept in.

"Keep your sweats on. You can change when we get back," Adam told the kids. "And take a sock or something small like that to use as a washcloth."

The three went out of the cave and down the hill toward the road. They heard another plane coming their way.

"Run!" Adam yelled. They ran uphill, as fast as they could, to get back into the cave. The plane circled around the mountain. Through the cave entrance, Adam could hear the sound grow louder every few minutes. They heard the plane overhead. He thought he could hear the plane coming back their way, so they waited until they could hear nothing. It was as if the plane might have ears too. Adam and the kids remained absolutely quiet, not even whispering, until the sound of the plane faded and did not return. Adam found himself shaking and realized he was more scared than he had thought. The thought of being a captive was overpowering. His imagination kept getting in the way of both his safety and his sanity.

They huddled just inside the cave opening and looked out at the daylight. Rain was beginning to fall through the fog, but it was a slow, drizzling rain. "Okay, guys, let's get our makeshift raincoats. Put on your jackets, and we'll go to the stream."

Adam went to the fire and added a few larger sticks, breaking up each one. He pulled a plastic bag over his head. The two kids watched him and did the same. They followed Adam down the mountain as soft raindrops hit their plastic coverings. Their feet stepped on the leaves covering the ground. The muffled sound lent a peaceful, eerie atmosphere to their surroundings.

They walked down the road--in no hurry to get where they were going. When they got to the old road, Adam didn't say anything. He just made the turn, and the two kids followed him. When they got to the little creek, he could see where he'd cleared out the creek and widened it.

He looked at Leila and said, "Put your clothes in the plastic so that you will be able to keep them dry. Luke and I will go down the creek a ways, and I'll help Luke. You holler at us when you are through."

Adam and Luke walked down the stream, looking for a wide spot where they could wash. Looking over his shoulder to make sure they were out of Leila's sight, Adam stopped. "We'll wash here, Luke."

Luke bent and trailed his fingers in the cold, clear water. His voice took on the half-crying, half-demanding tone that always caused Adam to grit his teeth. "But, I'm not washing here."

Adam responded, "If you don't, then your skin will get itchy. When you scratch, it will get infected."

He didn't insist. He just began taking off his clothes. Luke watched until Adam had completely shed not only his clothes, but also his shoes and socks. Making sure to magnify his motions, he carefully put his clothes, shoes, and socks into the plastic bag. Without saying anything, he walked into the water. It felt cold--colder than the day before. He got all the way into the water, then began pushing the sand aside and clearing out a wider area. When he had cleared out a small pool, he submerged himself all the way into the water. Like the day before, the cold--once he was out of the air--was not as bad.

"Come on, Luke," he yelled. He tried not to act as irritated as he really felt. Sometimes it was hard for Adam to tolerate Luke's whining, and he had to make himself remember that Luke was only six years old.

Dubious and in slow motion, Luke began to take off his clothes. He started by putting his jacket into the plastic bag--followed by his sweats, underwear, shoes, and socks--until all of his clothes were in the bag. He was already shivering. He pulled out his sock for washing and slowly put his feet into the water. His toes squished into the soft sand, and the water trickled up to his ankles.

"It's not too bad," he said. Then he slowly walked through the water to Adam.

Adam pulled his body all of the way under saying, "If you stay out of the air, it won't be as cold. Do you want me to help you wash so that you can keep under the water?"

Luke handed Adam the sock. "Would you?" Adam took the sock and scrubbed while Luke lay as low in the water as he possibly could.

Luke remained passive while Adam washed him. "Can I get out now?" Luke asked.

"I still need to wash myself. Can you please wait until I'm done so that I can help you get dry and into your clothes?"

Luke hunkered down in the water to stay out of the air while Adam washed with his sock.

To reassure Luke, he said, "This sure feels good."

While Luke watched Adam, he picked up pebbles from the stream bed and threw them into the brush bordering the stream.

He asked Adam, "Why does skin get itchy when you don't wash?"

Adam curbed his impulse to give Luke a sarcastic reply. He answered, "Old skin cells are constantly dying off, and most of them just stay there. Then, as they build up, they get itchy."

Luke looked at Adam thoughtfully, then scrubbed his arms and legs more thoroughly. Adam saw that Luke was always watching him and copying many of the things he did. Somehow, it made Adam feel older, and he couldn't help but like the feeling. He had always just stayed away from Luke because he was bothersome. Now he had to take care of the kid 24/7.

As Adam got out of the water, the cold air hit him and he couldn't help but suck in his breath from shock. "Come on, Luke, and I'll help you get some of the water off." Luke's little body was covered with huge chill bumps.

He helped Luke dry and held his arm to keep him balanced while he dressed. When Luke was finished and seated on a large rock, Adam shook off water and got dressed. He pulled on his plastic bag, which was already wet on the outside.

Luke looked up and said, "Thank you. I do feel better and, you were right, my skin was getting itchy."

Adam smiled at Luke in spite of himself. He found himself discovering that Luke was actually more than just some whiny little kid. Maybe he could help Luke find a way to be less whiny and less of a "Mama's boy." Adam stood very still and listened for Leila. He didn't hear a sound.

He yelled, "Leila, where are you?" There was no response. He yelled again.

"I'm freezing, but I'm okay."

"If you are still in the water, get out, and get yourself dried off."

"Just give me a few more minutes, Adam."

Adam and Luke sat down by the side of the little creek, watching the water. Every now and then, Adam could see water in mid-stream that was a little muddy. Water coming directly from where Leila had disturbed the water above them. He noted the rocks in the water, then remembered that he was going to get stones for making a type of fire place in the cave floor. The stones would help hold in the heat. His shoes were already on, so he'd have to get stones he could reach on land.

"Luke, help me get some stones for the fire."

Luke and Adam gathered stones and put them in Adam's extra plastic bag until they had several--at least, as many as Adam wanted to carry. As Adam put the last stone in his bag, he saw Leila coming back toward them. He hadn't heard her because the soft, wet leaves on the ground muffled the sound of her footsteps. Dampness coated everything. Tiny raindrops were still falling down, and Adam ran his hand through his hair, pushing out the excess water. Large drops flew from his head in a circle and Luke ducked.

In an effort to warm up a little bit, they walked back to the cave faster. Adam changed the sack of stones from one shoulder to the other. The sack seemed to get a little heavier, and more awkward, with each step. Finally, they could see the place to turn off toward the cave, and Adam was relieved.

His plan was that when they got back to the cave, they'd put the stones in a circle around where they had been building the fire, and use them to hold in the heat. Maybe they could cover up the hot coals with ashes and preserve the coals for the next fire. He was still thinking about this when they saw the cave entrance.

When they got inside, he set down the rocks and told the kids, "Use those stones to build some type of fireplace, then get us some more wood. I'm going to go down the road to see where it's cut off. Maybe Mom and Dad can still get back some way. We'll feel better when we know."

Adam really just wanted to be by himself for a while, and walking would help him unwind. It felt good to warm up after washing in the stream.

He walked back down the mountain to the road, and set out to see where the road was cut off. Maybe he wouldn't make it that far, but he just needed to figure out the real chances of his mom and dad returning.

He began walking back the way he'd come. The next time he walked, he'd go the other way and see what he could find. It was easier walking by himself, and he fully intended to go on at least one long walk each day--by himself!

He walked around a bend in the road. No longer worried about an oncoming car, he straddled the middle of the road. In three hours, he walked about six miles and was sweating under his raincoat trash bag. In the distance, Adam heard a low, steady sound coming through the trees. The noise was familiar, but the steady drizzle dampened it enough to make it unrecognizable. As muffled as it was, the noise seemed big, important. Adam hurried down the road, trying to see where the noise was coming from. He rounded a curve, and as the road straightened, he saw it disappear ahead of him. The road seemed to have completely fallen away. Adam approached the drop-off and stood frozen, watching the water.

Chapter 9 - Ocean Water

Adam lay down on the edge of the bank and placed his hands on the ground, sending loose rocks and dirt flying toward the water. He turned over onto his stomach to watch. The top of the bank was about as high as a two-story building and appeared unstable. He could barely see the opposite embankment. Adam didn't recognize the terrain on the other side. It looked different.

"How can Mom and Dad possibly get back to us?" he said out loud. For a while he just gazed at the water, mesmerized by its movement.

He tried to think about how this caved-in part of pavement had something to do with his parents not getting back. The only way his parents could return would be by boat. He could see that now. He wasn't sure how large the boat would have to be. What could he tell the kids? He wanted to give them some hope, so they would keep on trying. He also knew they would have to conserve their food. Adam tried to remember how long people could live without food, but he couldn't. He didn't want to find out either.

The water was turbulent and dirty and smelled like seawater. It flowed past quickly, almost like a river. The current was visible. Adam knew that the tide was either coming in or going out. Every now and then, a board, trash sack, or other debris flowed past the bank. He noticed signs of an earthquake and flooding as all kinds of branches, trees, roots, and parts of wood buildings floated past him.

As he watched, he saw a small dog with a black and brown head struggling in the water as it tried to get to solid ground. Adam imagined that people and other animals had probably struggled in the same way.

The little dog went under, struggled, then went under again. He wanted to help the little dog, but he was afraid to try to get all the way down the bank. He couldn't stand the thought of the little dog drowning. He didn't know how long the dog had been in the water, but he finally decided he had to try to save him. He didn't weigh the possible consequences.

Adam searched the ground and found a long stick. The stick was as thick as his wrist on one end and as narrow as his finger on the other. It was a lot longer than his six foot frame, so he grabbed it and sat down at the top of the bank. Holding onto the stick, he slid down the bank and pushed rocks out of his way. It seemed like he went faster and faster as he went down. He used his two feet as a braking mechanism. He hit the edge of the water with his feet, and he could still see the little dog. It was trying to get to the bank.

He yelled, "Come here, boy!"

The dog's head turned toward him. Adam pushed the tip of the stick out on the water toward the dog. The dog swam toward it, but went down again. Adam lost his grip on the stick. He yelled again, "Come on, come on."

The little dog went down again. When he surfaced, Adam saw that the current had pushed the dog and stick past him. The stick was gone. He walked along the edge of the water, stumbling as he kept pace with the dog. He yelled again, "Come on, come on!"

The current was pulling away from Adam. He had to think quickly, so he jumped into the turbulent water after the little dog. He hoped that the salt water would give him some buoyancy. He didn't have far to go, so he swam toward the little dog. The dog sank again and, for a moment, Adam couldn't see him. Then the dog bobbed back up. Adam grabbed and missed. He grabbed again and barely managed to grip one wet front paw. He pulled the dog as hard as he could toward him. Still in a panic, the dog put both paws on Adam's shoulders and kept up the swimming motions. Adam gripped the little dog with his left arm and swam with his right until he could stand at the edge of the water. The little dog hung on.

As Adam stood, water poured off both him and the little dog. He looked at the daunting sight of the unsteady dirt bank and knew that getting back up would not be easy. He tucked the little dog--still struggling for his life--inside his coat and tucked part of his coat inside the front of his pants. It seemed to calm down the little dog, but he still scratched Adam's stomach. He held onto the little dog, and the dog calmed down even more.

Adam began trying to get back up the bank on all fours. He got about halfway up, then started sliding back toward the water. He looked farther down the bank and saw that it was even steeper. He tried again, on all fours, and made it farther up the bank. He began slipping some and grabbed onto a large piece of asphalt sticking up out of the ground. He hung on, gasping for breath, while rocks and dirt slid down the bank behind him. He remembered from hiking that he could go at an angle to make getting up the hill easier. He stood up and tried again, but this time he went at a side angle toward another big chunk of asphalt sticking up out of the ground.

He focused on keeping his momentum. He knew that if he stopped, for even a second, he'd slip right back down. He went two steps and slipped back down one, up two, back one. He almost had to run to keep moving up the bank until he reached the edge of the bank. He grabbed the edge of the road and pulled as hard as he could, kicking his legs for an extra burst of speed upward. He landed on the road--on top of the dog. The little dog let out a yelp and wiggled free of Adam's clothes. Adam rolled onto his back and lay still, trying to catch his breath. They'd made it. He looked at the dog.

"Hello, there, little one."

The dog began wagging his tail and licking Adam's face. Smiling, Adam got up and started walking back toward the cave with the little dog following. He had about six miles to walk, and everything he was wearing was soaking wet, including his backpack. He searched in his pack for some jerky and found a piece that hadn't been opened. He broke off a little and gave it to the dog. The dog ate it like he hadn't eaten anything for a long time. He bit off a piece for himself and nibbled on it.

The little dog looked up at him, wagging his tail as if to say, "Can you give me some more?" Adam gave him another piece until, between them, they finished eating the meat. He didn't realize how cold he was until he began to shiver. He decided to walk back to the cave as fast as he could, so he would warm up faster. He quickened his pace and smiled as he remembered speed-walkers from a TV show he had watched before. The misty air began to stir and made his face colder even as his arms and legs began to warm. Even though it wasn't raining anymore, it remained cold. Adam could feel the *squish*, *squish* each time he put a foot on the ground. He had nothing to replace his soaked shoes and socks, so he just kept walking. He asked himself, "Why does it always seem like it's farther to get back than it was to get there?"

The road looked long and lonely, but he had the little dog and found him to be surprisingly good company. Adam began smiling as he pictured the looks on the kids' faces when he showed up at the cave with a little dog. He could just imagine Luke smiling. He walked even faster through the chilled air. The cold was cutting right through his thin, wet jacket, and shirt and pants. He wanted to get back to the dry cave before dark. He didn't think he could find his way back in the dark, especially from this angle. Oh, how he wanted to get back to the cave.

He thought about the little fire and wondered if the kids had started one again. He hoped they were careful with how many matches they used, but he knew that Leila was always careful. He could just see Luke going through a pile of matches, but she'd keep track.

He continued up the road, watching the shadows fill in the spaces between the trees. As he walked, the little dog trotted beside him. The dog seemed to be laboring to keep up. Adam scooped him up and carried him. Carrying the little dog seemed to help his own body warm up. He figured he'd walked about four or five miles since he gotten out of the water, and it was getting darker and darker.

He could walk down the road, but he knew he wouldn't be able to see where to turn off. He stopped and took off his backpack. Setting the backpack on the ground, he watched as the little dog bounced around-- suddenly more active. The little dog seemed to think he would be able to find some more jerky, but Adam knew he was out. He was surprised to find the inside of his pack partially dry. What a miracle.

"There is the flashlight, and it works!" Adam said speaking both to his new friend and to himself. He put the pack back on his shoulders and picked up the little dog with his left hand while he held the flashlight in his right hand. He had to watch for the place to turn off. *Maybe tomorrow I can place a rock to mark the trail up the mountain to the cave*, he thought.

He saw the place to turn, and was shining the light up the hill to be sure he had found the right place, when he heard a loud scream. It sounded like Luke. Gripping both the dog and the flashlight, Adam began running up the hill. He didn't even take the time to set the little dog onto the ground. He ran toward the cave. Toward Luke and Leila.

70

Chapter 10 - The Accident

As Adam got to the mouth of the cave, he heard Leila say, "Where is Adam? I want Adam!"

It sounded like she was about to cry. Though she had not shed one tear during the last few days. She had been a real trouper. Adam's heart began beating hard as he ducked inside the mouth of the cave.

Luke was on the ground with his shorts on, and there was a fire in a fireplace that the kids had put together. One side of the circle was missing. Adam bent down over Luke. "What happened, Luke?"

"We built the rocks to make a little fireplace, and then built a fire like you said. But one of the rocks exploded and cut into my leg."

Adam looked at the leg and saw that it was bleeding considerably. He knew they'd have to clean up the wounds so that Luke wouldn't get an infection. He had bought Band-Aids, but they were small, and he didn't have anything to kill bacteria. He backed toward the little fire.

Thinking out loud, he said, "All of us will have to be careful to wear pants anytime we are near the fire."

Adam looked the rocks over and noted that some of them were volcanic. He wasn't sure what kind of rock had exploded, but he was fairly certain that the rest of the rocks would be okay. He remembered from his Earth Science class that a rock exploding from water trapped inside was very rare. Of course one of those rare rocks would be one that had been brought to the cave for their fire.

"Luke, you are going to have to be real good because we are going to have to clean up your leg. Why are you in your shorts?"

Luke looked up at Adam with sorrowful eyes and said, "It was

71

getting warm."

Adam looked at frightened Leila and handed her the flashlight. Then, to distract Luke, he grabbed the little dog and said, "Look what I brought you, Luke. He will be your dog. How about that?"

"Wow! Can we keep him?"

"I don't see why not. I rescued him from the water. He is real hungry, so we will have to share our food with him."

"I'll share mine with him."

Luke began petting the little dog, which made his tail wag faster than ever. "Is he a puppy?"

"I don't think so. I think he is just a very small dog, and that is good because he won't eat very much."

By this time, Leila was also petting the little dog while she held the flashlight.

Adam got the cup and another sock. He told Luke to come outside the cave so they could scrub his leg without getting the cave floor wet. Adam knew they would have to keep the cave dry and clean.

He poured water on Luke's leg and scrubbed off the pieces of rock--except for one piece which was imbedded partially under the skin. He got that piece out with his fingers, causing it to bleed more than ever. Luke started crying. Adam had no idea how they were going to keep the deeper cut from getting infected . . . until the little dog came up to Luke and began licking his leg. Luke frowned and was going to push the dog away, but Adam remembered that dog's saliva has a natural antibiotic in it.

"Let the dog lick your leg anytime he wants. He'll keep it clean." He hugged Luke close and told him, "In fact, Luke, since the little dog is yours, you should get to name him."

"Really?" Luke asked, smiling. "He's spotted like black pepper. Can I name him Pepper?"

"I guess so," Adam said. "Are you sure? Anyway, let's get something to eat. I'm sure hungry. How about you guys?"

Leila heard and answered, "We were hungry while you were gone, so we ate some peanut butter and crackers. Can we give some to the dog?"

Leila had been scared while Adam was gone, and she was glad he was back. Adam cooked some macaroni and was careful around the little circle of rocks. Using a stick, he re-formed the rocks into a perfect circle. When the macaroni was cooked, he used the rest of the can of chili to help flavor it. Then, he cut up some cheese and added that to the macaroni. When he tasted it, he thought it wasn't half-bad. He was dividing up the food when he saw the little dog, Pepper, eating some peanut butter and crackers that Leila was giving him. Maybe he would be a pleasant addition to their little family.

After they finished eating, Adam got his beer. He was beginning to look forward to the beer each night. It helped him calm down. As he popped it open, he noticed that he had only two left. In reality, they really didn't have very much food left at all. Luke and Leila opened their pop and were sharing it. They had more pops than he had beer. It didn't seem fair, but then nothing seemed fair these days. It especially wasn't fair for him to be stuck taking care of two kids when he was just a kid himself. Adam felt that taking care of the little dog would help Luke be a little less whiney. The dog could also contribute by helping to keep Luke's leg from getting infected. While he sat next to the fire nursing his drink, his thoughts began to wander. He wondered how ancient people had discovered that a dog could keep a wound clean by licking it. He'd read about this several times. Luke really had hurt his leg, though, and the dog would help it heal. Adam wished he had something to read, and he wished they had more food. He also wished he didn't have to babysit.

Thinking about food made Adam realize that he would have to go look for more tomorrow. Maybe he would be better off if he left the kids at home this time because he would be gone at least overnight. He went back inside the cave, got his backpack, and put it close to the heat of the fire so that it would dry completely. The rocks helped hold in the heat and would help his pack dry up. He'd have to get things ready for tomorrow so that he could leave the minute the first sunlight showed at the cave entrance. He could make faster progress without the kids.

He made some crackers and peanut butter, packed one of his last two beers, got the flashlight, and filled the coffee cup with water. He'd wear his jacket when he started out, but he would put it in his backpack later when he got warm. Also, he'd make sure that his "raincoat" trash sack was packed along with a couple of extra trash sacks. That way he could carry anything he found. Getting food for them was a problem which could get critical really soon.

Adam wondered what his father had been thinking. Maybe

they'd have been better off just staying in their house and doing their best, like other people.

Adam finished up his beer, still checking to make sure he had everything ready for the trip the next day. Then he remembered the little folding shovel. He wondered, *Should I take the shovel?* It would take up space in his backpack, and he might not need it. He decided to take it, so he put it in the pile of things ready to go.

"Can we listen to the radio again?" asked Leila. He'd forgotten about the radio, and they had only a few days left of being able to get news in English. They turned it on, and it was playing Spanish music.

"You know, I kind of like this type of music. It has such a bouncy rhythm to it." Leila said. They all sat down waiting for the nightly news that they had found on the radio.

"You are listening to the English version of KDLA, which will be broadcast until November 10. After that time, all radio and other forms of communication will be in Spanish--the official language of the Alliance. Any person attempting to communicate in any other language will be fined. This is the Democratic Latin Alliance, Station 55.

"Since the goal is for everyone to be equal in a true democratic society, Indian reservations will be absorbed, but Native Americans will get to keep any lands deeded to individuals. Collective lands will belong to the Alliance. If there is anyone left on the island of *El Quarto,* they will be evacuated to other places or work camps. There will be no residents on the island because there will be no ferry runs. The Alliance cannot afford the expense of maintaining the island. All cities along the coast were destroyed in the earthquake, and we have combed the island for survivors and evacuated them to the mainland. Seattle, Bremerton, Port Angeles, Aberdeen, and similar cities along the waterway are now under water. Shelton is partially destroyed and under water as well. If you know of any people who need rescuing, let the radio station know. This concludes our English broadcast for today. Stay tuned tomorrow for news and instructions."

"Wow!" Luke said. "What will people do when there are no more English radio or TV stations?"

"Well, I guess they'll listen in Spanish and just get used to it."

"Will that be hard?" Luke asked.

"I just don't know. I took Spanish in school, but I only know a

74

few words. I guess I can always learn, but let's hope the United States gets back together before we have to find out."

"Do you think that will happen?" Leila asked.

"All we can do is hope, and wait for Mom and Dad. I'm certain that they'll find a way of getting back here if they're okay. Tomorrow, I'm going to go out by myself and search for more food for us while you guys stay here and wait for Mom and Dad."

The next day, he'd travel alone, and let the kids stay at the cave. Luke could keep Pepper, so that he wouldn't follow Adam. He sure didn't want to deal with the little dog when he was hiding from the helicopter men, but he was still glad that he rescued him. He just couldn't stand it when the little dog had looked at him--then went under water. He would never regret saving him. He thought, *Tomorrow will be another day*.

Chapter 11 - The Journey

The dimmest ray of light hit the cave entrance and enticed Adam to get up. He picked up his backpack, which wasn't quite dry yet, and carefully placed all of his things from the pile inside his pack. Pepper greeted him by asking for something to eat, so Adam gave him a cracker with peanut butter. They had plenty of peanut butter but not very much of anything else.

Adam decided that he would boil some eggs. He would leave some for the kids to eat and take some with him for the next day. He had no idea just what he would encounter, and he couldn't afford to light a fire while he explored. That would make him an easy target, and he would be certain to be discovered.

To boil his eggs, he got some dry leaves and carefully pushed back some of the ashes with a little stick. Then he placed just a few dry leaves on top of the coals, watching the smoke gradually increase. It looked like it was going to go out, so he blew carefully into the coals. A tiny spark caught and grew on the leaves. He blew some more. He kept blowing--easy--until the leaves caught fire. He placed small twigs on top, then carefully placed more and larger twigs until he had a little fire. He got the pan and put in some eggs. He went to the mouth of the cave and caught enough water in the pan to cover the eggs. He set the pan against the rocks and nestled it against the ground so that it wouldn't spill. By this time, the kids were up and sat down to watch the eggs boil.

"We don't have any salt," Leila said. "I don't want to eat boiled eggs without salt."

"You know what, Leila, if you don't want to eat anything, then don't. I'm sure not going to make you eat. I'm not your mother."

Adam was irritated. Here, he'd gotten the fire going without using any matches and was fixing something for them to eat, and all Leila could think about was the lack of condiments. He wanted to kick something, but he remembered the last time that he kicked something, he'd only hurt his foot. He made himself think about the fact that he'd be leaving soon, and they would just have to take care of themselves. Adam couldn't wait.

Luke kept on his shorts and was letting Pepper lick his leg. Adam looked closely at Luke's leg to make sure there wasn't a sign of infection. The leg looked great considering their lack of supplies. They were well-sealed over with scabs. He smiled to himself. Pepper was already earning his keep.

Adam watched the eggs boil for a while. He had no idea just how long to cook eggs. He let them boil while he rearranged his things in the backpack. When he decided the eggs might be cooked, he went outside and poured out the hot water. When they had cooled, he took three of them.

"You guys can eat what you want, but these eggs will give you some protein. Just make sure that you don't pig out because I may not even be able to find any kind of food. If I'm not back by dark, just get ready for bed, but you can listen to the radio for a while. Luke, you hold Pepper until I've been gone for a while so that he will stay with you. Bye, guys."

He put on his jacket, threw his backpack over his shoulder, and headed down the mountain toward the road.

His plan was to walk toward Aberdeen, even though that area, according to the radio, was now under water. There had been some isolated homes on the way to Aberdeen. Maybe there would be some food left behind. They could use almost anything.

Adam walked to the road, then followed the same route he'd taken when he found Pepper. He found the place where the road had caved in and made sure that he stayed a good distance away from the edge. By keeping the edge just visible, Adam found that he could walk in the partial clearing without danger of falling. His progress was easy and fast. He watched the fog as it gradually faded into the distance before completely disappearing. It began to warm up as he walked, and after a couple of hours, he took off his red and black letterman jacket and packed it away.

His path gradually led away from the edge of the broken road. Long after the sound of running water had faded, he saw a lake through the trees. As he approached the lake, he could see the roof of a large house. The closer he got to the house, the larger it appeared. He would have to walk the entire distance around the lake in order to get to the house. He wondered if someone would be inside it. What would he find? The more questions he came up with, the faster he walked. He walked past a concrete picnic table near the shore of the lake and decided to sit down for a while. The day was getting to be really warm. There was a fresh smell of grass and trees, yet it still smelled slightly of the dampness of fog.

He looked toward the house, then couldn't resist getting back up and hurrying around the lake. It intrigued him a little, scared him a little, and gave him some hope of finding some more food for himself, the kids, and Pepper. He walked as close to the shore as he could and kept his eyes on the distant house while watching in all directions for any sign of another person. What would he find?

When he got within a hundred feet of the house, he stopped and listened. He heard the *chee-chee* of a squirrel and the mixed sounds of birds, but nothing larger. He listened harder. He took a few steps and stopped. He listened some more. The forest sounds in the backdrop of the quiet were reassuring. He was listening so hard that he could hear the *crunch* of each step his feet took. *Crunch, crunch, chee-chee, crunch, crunch.* He stopped and listened some more. He got closer to the front door of the house and hid behind a tree. He picked up a small rock and threw it toward the house. It hit with a *kelunk*! The birds stopped singing, the squirrel hushed, and there was only silence.

He walked up to the front porch and tried the door. It was not locked like the ranger cabin had been, and it opened easily. Adam peered through the doorway. He scanned the scene for a moment, then stepped inside.

Inside, he saw a general state of disorder. It felt kind of weird looking inside someone's house when no one was even there. Clothes were strewn around the living room floor next to several suitcases. It looked like someone had been disrupted while packing.

He went toward the back of the house, looking for the kitchen. By the door to the kitchen, he saw a telephone and couldn't help picking it up. The line was dead. He punched the numbers in but got nothing. He even tried 911, but there was nothing.

"I guess there is no more 911," he said out loud. He went into the kitchen and saw plates on the table, along with some kind of gross-looking, dried-up food. He went to the refrigerator and found some pops, a couple of cartons of eggs, and butter. Then he went to the cabinets and threw them open one-by-one. He went back to the fridge and got a pop, opened it, and sat down at the table while he surveyed the contents of the cabinets. He was mentally planning what he could carry back to the cave.

As he sat there, he thought he heard something. He sat still, listening carefully. He heard the unmistakable *whine-thump* sound of a helicopter. The sound grew louder and higher pitched as if the craft were going to land. The combination of sounds filled Adam with fear. Men were coming. He quickly prepared to hide just in case. He ran around the kitchen closing the cabinet doors and the refrigerator door. He went into the adjoining bathroom and hid behind the door. The helicopter had not yet landed, but he didn't quite feel safe. He ran back to the dining area and ducked out a broken window. He ran to the end of the deck and crawled under it--clear to the edge of the foundation on the house. Green ferns were growing under the deck. They crowded into his face, which improved his chances of remaining hidden. He scrunched behind a large clump of the ferns and tight against the foundation of the house. The cold from the concrete felt somehow comforting against the skin on his face.

The helicopter landed, and he heard the rotors slowing down. Adam was shaking so hard, he thought he'd pass out, but he just lay there motionless. It sounded like two men got off the helicopter, and they were speaking Spanish. Adam caught a few words like "*no gentes*" and "*gringos*." All he could do was lie there and pray they wouldn't look under the house. His heart started beating harder, then he remembered that he left the opened pop sitting on the table. The pop had been room temperature, so they would have no idea how long the pop might have been opened. But it would still fizzle. He shook as he lay there worrying. If they looked in the can of pop, they would notice it still had fizz. His fear increased as he heard footsteps throughout the house. He heard more talking as the men stepped onto the deck. It seemed like they were stepping right over Adam. He heard some more talking, and then he heard them going down the deck steps. What a relief! Were they going to look under the deck? It didn't sound like they even went into the kitchen.

Adam thought that they may have been turned off by the general mess in the kitchen. He relaxed a bit as he heard them step off the deck and keep walking. They were laughing and talking about "*gringos perezoso*." They walked around the house and toward the woods. Their voices faded. He huddled under the deck of the house. He was so thankful that he was alone that he said a prayer of thanks right then. Pepper would have given him away.

It seemed like forever until the men quit talking and walking around. Apparently they went back to the helicopter because he didn't hear them reenter the house. With a great feeling of relief, Adam pulled off his backpack, took out the beer, and used the backpack to prop up his head. He wasn't going to move from his hiding place for a long time, maybe not until dark. He sipped his warm beer slowly and felt himself relaxing.

The whole day had been a bit much, but as he thought back over it, one thing he was thankful for was the broken-out window in the dining room. He fell asleep against the cold of the concrete foundation under the deck of the house.

When Adam woke up, it was dark and quiet. No birds were chirping, no little critters were chattering, and there was no wind. Not a sound. He crawled from underneath the deck, pausing every couple of seconds to listen for the men's return. He was surprised how long it took for him to make it out from under his temporary cover. It had seemed so small when he was ducking under it for cover. It had served him well, and the men had not found him.

There were a few cans and packages of food in the kitchen, so he decided that he'd pack up everything he could carry and head out early the next day. He went inside the living room. The couch was still against the wall. He pushed away the clothes that were covering it, lay down, and stretched out. It felt good to stretch out on something so comfortable for once. Adam had never thought much about sleeping on a couch before, but after spending several nights in a cave, he could appreciate the couch. He fell asleep again, listening and wary of any new sounds. There was nothing to disturb him, and it felt so good. So very good.

80

Adam's sleep was interrupted by the sound of the helicopter retuning. He jumped off the couch when he heard it land, and he began running for the back door and the patio. When he got to the back door, he paused. The night was quiet. He opened the door and walked around the side of the house. Everything was still. In the bushes nearby, birds started to sing. He noticed that the sky was starting to turn grey as daylight approached. Adam shook his head and remembered how frightened the men had made him. Now he was dreaming about them! He thought about the kids, and he wanted to get back to the cave. He hoped Luke's leg was still healing okay. With Pepper's help, it would. Still nervous, he went back inside the house.

He removed the boiled eggs from his backpack. He peeled each one slowly--being careful to place the shells into his backpack. The men might come back, and he couldn't leave any evidence that he'd been there. He got his bottle of water and drank it, then reopened the cabinets and grabbed all of the canned goods, packages of beans, and macaroni. He glanced inside the refrigerator and got the butter. It might not be good anymore, but they could use the fat. He opened the top freezer, hoping to find something that could be salvaged. Melted ice cream had made a mess, but there was cheese that looked like it had mold on it. Adam knew that mold serves as a natural preservative for cheese, so he took both sealed chunks. He opened the bottom cabinets and found some liquid soap, laundry soap, and potatoes in a twenty-pound sack. Some of the potatoes were bad, but he took them anyway. He decided to leave the laundry soap because it was in a really large, heavy box. He could return and get it later.

He went into the bathroom and found some wash rags--still folded. He took all of them as well as three towels. In order to save space, he only got one for each of them. When he put the things together into the trash sack, he decided that he'd split his goods into two sacks to equalize the weight. Maybe it would be easier to carry. After he got well away from the house, he would sort out things. He was anxious to get out of that house and back into the woods where it was easier to hide.

He carefully assessed the kitchen and made sure everything looked the same. He made sure all of the cabinets were closed. He stopped to be still and listen every few seconds. This place spooked him. He stood and listened several times, then decided that listening would just delay his exit from the house. So he went to the drawers in the kitchen--looking for a can opener and a knife or two. He found both. They were in a small drawer. He dumped the contents of the drawer into his backpack. He wedged two larger steak knives in the frame of his pack. The last thing he needed was to cut himself. He got the wash rags and crammed them in with the cooking things.

He went through the living room, glanced around, and found a small stack of magazines and about a half dozen books. He grabbed the books and stuffed them in a sack. Then, after he was sure that everything looked okay, he put his backpack on his back, balanced one sack on each shoulder, and headed out. On the way out, Adam found a wood chopping block with a small hatchet and a large ax. He decided he'd take the smaller hatchet. The large ax felt heavy, and he would rather keep more food than carry the ax. He fit the hatchet easily into his backpack.

Adam headed right into the woods. This time he decided he would skirt the tree line so he could hide more quickly if he heard the helicopters again. He walked about a mile, then stopped under a tree to rearrange his new goods. The first thing he did was get out the potatoes and remove the bad ones. Then he pulled out the cheese with the mold. He discovered that the mold was only on the outside of the cheese package, and it seemed to have been caused by the melted ice cream. He wiped it off with one of the wash rags. To his surprise, he discovered that he had a box of salt and a little sack of sugar. He was happiest about the salt. There were also three large boxes of tea. He wasn't a tea drinker, but he decided he might learn to be one. By some stroke of luck, the mist was light that morning, and Adam didn't even bother with his coat. He'd just get hot later.

When he had opened the refrigerator, he had decided to leave the pops in case those two men came back. He had only the rest of his water to drink. He decided to leave everything, take a good drink, and refill his water bottle in the lake. The two men had obviously been looking for their "*gringos perezoso*." They might be back. He didn't want them to suspect anything. He sat down pensively, watching in the direction of the house. He could just barely see it. He hurried because the little lake was in a clearing, and he knew now that he should avoid walking in clearings.

After he filled his bottle, he returned to his bags. He took a brief rest against a tree stump, shouldered his backpack, picked up the sacks, and began walking. He felt tired, so he didn't walk very fast. He hadn't used his flashlight much, so he figured he'd be able to find his way back if it got dark on him. For some reason, walking back was less interesting than heading out to see what he could find. It seemed that every time Adam went out, he ended up with something new. It intrigued him.

Going back over the same ground, however, would have been boring if it weren't for the fact that he was still scared and wary. Thank goodness he'd left Pepper back with the kids. Adam hoped the kids were doing okay. As he thought of them, he remembered how Leila had commented on the lack of salt for the eggs. He wondered whether she had eaten any. At least he knew the kids were safe. He'd cautioned them about pigging out and about saving food so that it would stretch out until they could get out of the cave and get back home--whenever that would be. After walking about five miles, he realized that he was hungry and remembered his crackers and peanut butter. The light mist had stopped just as he thought it would. He decided to take a full break and sit down for his meal. He walked until he found a large tree. He took a few seconds to scrape away the damp needles and settled down to eat.

He rested a bit, then dozed off until he heard a sound in the woods that sounded like brush breaking. Remembering the men from the day before, Adam held still as he listened. After a few seconds, the woods were quiet. Adam edged closer to the tree, then paused to listen again. In the clearing in front of him, he saw a small black bear, barely visible through a clump of bushes. He tightened himself against the tree and watched the bear. The bear was still a ways away, but it startled him. He didn't move. He waited for another several minutes. The bear was moving away from him. He listened as the sound of the bear gradually diminished. Finally, he headed in the direction of the cave. His mission was to get to the cave as fast as he possibly could.

Chapter 12 - Examining Loot

Adam fatigued quickly. With a sack on each shoulder, he didn't have any way to shift the weight and give his muscles a rest. He finally got back to the place where he'd found Pepper. Discovering his hunger and finding a clump of tall trees, Adam sat down. Most of the things that he had found had to be cooked, but he still had a few crackers with peanut butter. He ate those, drank almost all of his water, and rested again. It was early afternoon, and all the fog had lifted. The sun shone through the clouds for a while. He loved the combination of sunshine and blue sky.

He watched the water for a while from a distance. It seemed like the current wasn't quite as turbulent as before, and he didn't see anything unusual floating around in it. He found himself worrying about the kids but couldn't really understand why. It felt so good to finally be by himself for a bit. Taking care of kids was not a job that he had chosen. Maybe that was why it bugged him so much. He had not asked for the job. He looked out over the water and thought about his parents. Would they get back to them? He had no real reason to believe that they were even still alive. Were they? Was their house under water? Thinking about these things made Adam weary, and he just wanted to be safe and secure in the little cave with the kids and Pepper. He put the almost-empty water bottle back in the backpack, picked up each large trash sack, and began walking toward the cave.

When he had first started off, he had walked as fast as he could. But after four or five more miles, his steps slowed. He didn't hear any more helicopters, and he didn't see any more large animals. For that,

Adam was glad. The sun felt really warm on his face and shoulders, and the air was fresh and getting crisp with the coming moisture of evening. He wanted to get back before nightfall.

After walking for a while, he found the place where he had to turn off the road toward the cave. He quickened his steps, hurrying up the mountain. All of a sudden, he heard the little dog barking. He had to smile because it showed that Pepper considered the cave home, and he was protecting his home. The dog had already proven himself to be useful for Luke's leg, and now he was trying to protect his cave home.

Adam finally arrived at the mouth of the cave. He stepped inside, shed his sacks, and pulled off his backpack. What a relief! Luke ran to him first and gave him a big hug. "I'm glad you are back. It's more scary when you are gone."

Leila said, "You'll never guess what the radio said."

"What did the radio say?"

"They said that there would be no school after sixth grade. The only people who can go to school will be the ones who can get the highest scores on a test."

"But what will kids do after the sixth grade? Did they say?"

"Yes, they said that any kid who was out of sixth grade would work in the work camps. They said that most high school buildings would be used as a place for kids to stay while working."

Adam sat down, absorbing the startling news. It was a lot to take in. He looked at Leila and tried to imagine her, at 12, working in a work camp. He imagined what could happen to her, and all of a sudden, he was glad that they had remained hidden. He couldn't stand the thought of Leila not getting to go to school. She had always loved school so much, especially reading and math. This new life, no matter where a person lived, was definitely going to be much harder than the old one. Thinking of reading reminded Adam about the reading material he'd found. He missed having something to read.

He told Leila, "Guess what? I found some reading materials. There are some books and some magazines."

"Can we look at them?" Leila asked.

Adam got up and walked over to the two sacks, rummaging into each until he found the books and magazines. There were two women's magazines, a Bible, a dictionary, two children's books, and a newer-looking Spanish textbook that Adam recognized as having come from

85

a high school. It hadn't been used very much, but he knew they would use it now. Both children's books were a little young for the kids, but they would read them anyway.

He was glad to find the Bible because it contained familiar stories, and he would be able to spend time reading to the kids.

"There's not much here to read," Leila said, disappointed.

"That's true, Leila, but look. Here is a Spanish book. We can all learn some Spanish."

Luke whined, "But I don't want to learn Spanish. Why should I learn it?"

"It would be very smart to learn it because when you hear people talking, you will know what they are saying. But that will be only if you know the language."

"But I don't want to know what they are saying," Luke pouted.

"Let me tell you a story about what happened to me, okay?"

The three kids sat down around the little fire--with Luke and Leila gazing toward Adam expectantly.

"Well, I was in this house where I found these things when I heard a helicopter, so I jumped through a broken window and hid under the deck in case the men in the helicopter came into the house. They are looking for any people left on the island, and they want the island to be uninhabited."

Luke asked, "What does 'uninhabited' mean?"

"It means 'not lived in.'"

Adam went on with his story, "Anyway, they landed the helicopter and checked in the house, but they didn't do a very good job because I had left an opened pop on the table, and they only walked through the kitchen to get outside to the deck. While they were in the house walking around, I kept hearing them say the word "*pelizoso*" each time they said "*gringo*." I didn't know what that meant, and I still don't know."

Leila asked, "Were you scared?"

"I was so scared that I stayed there until it got dark, which was way after I heard the helicopter leave. From now on, when we go somewhere, we have to make sure that we are always close to the woods so that we can hide among the trees. Let's turn on the radio so that when they make their little talk in English, we will hear what they have to say. I guess we will only get English on the radio for a little while yet. We have to be careful how we use the radio because we don't have any

86

batteries to replace the ones already in it."

"Isn't it great that I bought you that radio last Christmas?"

"It sure is, Luke."

Adam went over to the area where they put the radio, then he noticed that things were quite messed up.

"What happened here?" he asked.

Leila answered, "Pepper tore open the package of crackers and ate a whole bunch of them. I spanked him and put them up as high as I could."

"Well, I saw a bear on my trip, so I guess we have to be more careful with food."

Adam saw Pepper nosing around the new sacks. He went to the large trash can and emptied it. "This will now be our food storage bin. It will be a bit of work getting what we want out, but it will keep our food safer. We'll put everything in it except the canned goods."

Leila asked, "What is in the new sacks?"

"Well, I really don't know. The only thing that I can remember is that there is a pizza mix. Maybe we'll try that tonight."

Luke was suddenly excited, "Yeah, pizza!"

"Before you get excited, remember that we don't have an oven, and no matter what we do with the mix, it won't be like pizza as you know it. Don't get too excited, and you won't be too disappointed. That always helps me keep from being angry and upset. I just don't expect too much."

"I'll try."

Adam noticed that this time he hadn't started with that annoying word "*but*."

Leila had gone to the sacks and was removing the items one at a time. She was curious. Adam gathered up the cans of food and lined them up against the cave wall. That way they could see what they had. He decided that they would just have to put the eggs on the very top of the trash can storage unit--under the lid. They had no way to keep them cool, so those eggs would have to be eaten right away.

He turned on the radio so they could listen to music until the short English broadcast came on the air. Leila found the box labeled "Pizza Mix" and happily showed it to Luke.

Adam asked, "How can we cook it?"

Leila said, "Mom always makes pizza by making the crust first.

But like you said, we have no oven, and Mom always cooks it in the oven."

"We have a cast iron skillet. Maybe we can make the pizza anyway. Let's try."

Adam took the package from Leila and used a pan to make the crust mix. He only had to add water. The recipe said one cup of water, so he guessed on the amount and poured it in while he stirred. He let it rise, then he went to the other sack and got out the package of butter and a block of cheese. He used a small amount of butter on the bottom of the skillet. He spread the crust over it, patted it down, and pushed the dough from the middle to the edges. He got a towel, folded it, and placed it over the skillet--being careful to make the folds fit the skillet closely so that the towel didn't catch on fire. "

Now," he said, "we have an oven. Let's see what else we have to do." According to the package, he just had to pour on the sauce and open the little packet of dried cheese to put on top.

Smiling, Adam got out the can opener from his backpack. "Look what else we have now."

He opened the slender can. Then, he waited until the skillet was hot and the crust was looking at least a little bit cooked. He poured on the sauce, added the dried cheese, then opened the block of cheddar and sliced some on top of the pizza. He covered the whole thing with the towel again. After a while, the pizza smelled really good. It was going to be their best meal yet.

Adam felt good. They were beginning to get the hang of things.

He peeked into the skillet and decided to let it cook some more. Finally, he took the skillet off of the fire and set it on the ground. He let it set for a while to continue cooking while he got a knife out of the backpack. He took the towel off the pizza, cut it into six slices, and put two slices on each plate. He thought that if Luke didn't like it, he would get his leftovers. In a way, he hoped Luke didn't want his. The smell of the pizza made him hungry. Pepper was bouncing around like he knew that he was going to eat.

"Everyone needs to give Pepper a little of theirs, so that he gets to eat too," he told the kids.

The kids opened their pop and sat down to eat their pizza. The thick part around the edges was not quite cooked, but Adam didn't care. It was food, and it was fresh-cooked. What an improvement over peanut butter and crackers.

"This crust is yucky," Luke said.

Leila was eating hers like it was the first meal she'd had for a very long time. "Then give your crust to Pepper or give me the whole thing. I don't care. Can't you ever stop whining? Do you know how tiresome it is to listen to you forever whining?"

Luke just looked at Adam and broke off his crust and gave it to Pepper. He didn't answer his brother. Adam found himself getting angry at him again, and he went to his pile of things and got out his beer. After he finished it, he had only one left. He could use it after his experiences over the last two days. Beer and pizza. Man, you can't get any better than that, even if the beer wasn't all that cold--or good.

He told the kids, "What good is whining anyway? Whining doesn't fix anything."

Leila grinned at Adam. "I don't whine."

"Thank goodness," he said.

In the middle of their meal, the music cut off, and the broadcast came on.

"Good evening, ladies and gentlemen. It is now October 27th, and we have exactly one week left before all communication will be in Spanish. We hope that you will learn the language. The Democratic Latin Alliance will be a one-language nation. Work crews are beginning to get some of the rubble cleared after the earthquake, and we are seeing some progress. The island of *El Quarto* has been vacated, but we are still sending helicopters into the region to rescue anyone who may have been left on the island. It is our plan to use the island for conservation, and let it go back to nature. The Democratic Latin Alliance is environmentally-friendly and will work to preserve nature. Again, any of you who wish to exchange any of your money into Latin pesos, you can exchange two U.S. dollars for one Latin dollar. All money currently in banks has already been exchanged, and owners of accounts will find the adjustment with their new statement. This concludes our broadcast for today. *Hasta la vista los gentes perezoso todos.*"

The three of them sat, silently looking at each other and taking in what had been said. Adam got up without saying a word and turned off the radio. He was more sure than ever that they should remain hidden. Maybe their parents would find a way of getting out here when things settled down. That is, if they were still alive.

Adam's thoughts returned to the broadcast. There, again, was that word that he didn't know: "*perezoso*." He realized that the word was also used with the word "gringo" and in a derogatory way. He said out loud, but mostly to himself, "What does it mean?"

Adam went to one of the sacks that was still on the cave floor. He took out the Spanish book and looked for that word *perezoso*. He found it, then it made sense. The word meant *lazy*. So, they were calling his kind of people "lazy, white men" just because they weren't willing to work for free for the Democratic Latin Alliance. Adam knew that he wasn't lazy, but he also knew that if he were in a work camp, he'd be reluctant to work to the best of his ability. No one wanted to be forced to do something.

Chapter 13 - Cave Work

The next morning, the misty fog rose almost to the entrance of the cave. It was a day to get the cave organized and fix up their belongings so that they could keep better track of what they had. Adam made scrambled eggs again. This time, he used a small amount of fat and added some salt and chunks of cheese. The eggs turned out so much better, even Luke didn't complain. Pepper had eaten quite a bit of the crackers, but there was a whole unopened box left, so at least they still had crackers. That evening, Adam planned to experiment with cooking the potatoes. He'd read in a book once that men on a camping trip had covered potatoes with mud and cooked them on the edge of the fire until they were done. It sounded good to him, and that would be what they would cook for supper. They could even add some cheese and salt. It already made him hungry. In his imagination, he could just about taste them, but they would wait until that night. He knew they'd eat the potatoes even if they weren't all that good. They were all learning that food didn't have to be perfect for it to be something to eat and for it to stop the hunger.

He found the little hatchet and used the flat area behind the blade as a hammer. He chipped away some nooks in the cave wall--toward the back of the cave where it was dry. It took a long time to get them chipped away. When he was finished, he put the knives up on them. He was making sure that they were up high. He made another little ledge for the can opener, but at a height just right for Luke to reach. With the dog and Luke, it seemed safer to keep those things up off the ground. Adam thought it looked neater too. He liked his things neat, and he

91

hated his belongings to appear chaotic and disorganized.

Leila, Adam noticed, was really pitching in to help with organizing things. He liked the way she always looked for constructive ways to fix things up. It seemed like she also knew just how to keep from making him angry. Luke, however, seemed to deliberately try to antagonize him. Adam tried thinking back to when he was younger. He didn't think that he'd been whiny like Luke, but then he hadn't been babied by his parents either. Well, there sure wasn't time for babying here.

Adam couldn't see Luke surviving in this new world unless he could change. If he put all of his energy into antagonizing Adam just to make him angry, it would sure be a waste because Adam didn't intend to lose his temper and harm himself anymore. It seemed like every time he got angry, he ended up getting hurt himself. His foot was still stiff, and it ached on nights after he'd been walking a lot. Surviving in this new world depended on being fit and industrious. They had amassed a lot of things, but it seemed like they didn't have many of the right things.

Adam gave Luke and Leila each a towel. Leila was excited about having her own towel.

He told the kids, "We'll have to dry them inside the cave during the winter. I'm not sure how we can do that, but we'll never get them dry outside until summer. Maybe by then there won't be anymore helicopters, and Mom and Dad will have returned." The last statement he had added for the sake of giving Luke and Leila something to hang onto.

"Let's go to the creek and wash up. I have a little soap now, and we have washrags and towels. I can't wait." The kids were only too glad to follow Adam to the creek. After they got outside, they noticed that the air in the cave had become stifling and smoky smelling, but the air outside was fresh and smelled like cedar.

"Can we take a cedar bough back with us and put it on the fire to make the cave smell better?" Leila asked.

"I don't know why not. I think that would be a great idea."

When they got to the creek, Adam gave Leila some soap. Then she walked above the boys, so that she could take off all of her clothes this time. She couldn't wait to wash her hair, even if the water was colder than before. As they expected, once they were submerged, it wasn't so bad. Adam had been washing when he saw soap suds trickling down from up the stream, and he knew that Leila was probably washing her hair. The bubbles gravitated toward the main flow of water, and he watched them for a while, mesmerized, as they floated on down the stream undisturbed.

"Luke, do you want me to help you wash your hair?" Adam asked him, hoping that he wouldn't hear any whining.

Luke answered, "Will it be cold?" Adam was pleased that he hadn't started his sentence with his favorite word, "but." And he didn't whine.

"It will be cold, but now you have a towel, so you can get dry easier."

"Okay," Luke said.

Adam washed Luke's hair for him and made sure all of the soap was rinsed out. Then he washed his own hair. He couldn't keep his head under water, which made him colder than ever. Afterward, both boys climbed out of the water, wrung out their washcloths, and dried as fast as they could. Luke shook so hard from the cold, he could hardly use his hands. Pepper got out of the water when they did and shook his whole body--sending water in every direction. Hurrying to get their clothes back on, they just ignored him.

Adam yelled to Leila, "We're out of the water now and dressed."

After she answered back, they sat down to wait for her. Adam noticed that the mist had quit, and it looked like it would really be a sunny day. He didn't want to spend the day in the cave, so he decided that he would spend some time getting more wood. While he sat there, he absentmindedly tossed a large stick into the water. Pepper plunged into the stream and brought the stick back to him.

"Look what Pepper did!" Luke said, smiling. Luke didn't smile very much, so Adam thought that a smile was a sign of improvement.

All of a sudden, Pepper began barking and barking. Luke and Adam ducked into the trees as fast as they could to hide, even though they had no idea what they might be hiding from. Pepper kept barking. The two boys were hidden behind the trees when Leila came into the clearing, laughing at Pepper. She began looking for the boys, so they decided they'd stay hidden for a while to see if she could find them. Pepper started wagging his tail wildly and ran up to Leila when he spotted her. Then, he went directly to the boys, so there really was no game for Leila to find them.

"Why are you hiding?" she asked.

"Because we didn't know what Pepper was barking at, and we forgot that he might bark at you. He's a good barker, isn't he?" Adam said.

He realized that since he had brought Pepper back to the cave, the kids had something to talk about besides the invasion, the earthquake, or their parents. Pepper's antics had brought them smiles and laughter when they needed them. And, he just might save them sometime by giving them a good warning. On the other hand, his barking might just do the opposite and draw attention to them. Adam thought that he'd need to teach Pepper to be quiet when commanded. It was something they would all have to work on.

When they got back to the cave, Adam got the small hatchet. He wished he'd been able to get the larger ax but finding something to burn wouldn't be too hard in these woods. He went out of the cave and up the mountain this time. He didn't want to create a visible disruption of the woods in case the helicopters were still searching. On the radio, they made it sound like they were rescuing people, but somehow Adam didn't believe that. The new government didn't want to put much into cleaning up after the earthquake. It worried him what might happen to Leila if they were found. Adam didn't know whether they would let the three of them stay together. He wondered how long it would take for the United States Government to get back control. He had no doubt that they would soon be back in control of the nation.

Adam took Pepper with him into the woods. Pepper could warn him if some other creature was nosing around while he was getting some wood. He thought about the bear from the day before. The last thing he wanted was to be attacked by a bear. What if they were living in a bear's cave, and the bear came back to hibernate for the winter? It was the first time he thought about that possibility.

He didn't want to get too far away from the cave because he still wanted to get some things straightened up inside it. One thing was for sure, they couldn't risk having an animal, or Pepper, get into their food.

Adam had heard that bears could bite through a can, but he wasn't sure if that was true. They would just have to take that risk because there wasn't enough room in the plastic garbage can for their cans of food too. Leila had stacked the peanut butter and jelly up against the wall in a neat order, and Adam was glad.

He felt that chopping some wood would warm him up, and he was itching to get his muscles moving. He found a downed tree which was about the diameter of his leg. The tree was covered with moss that looked like it might have been there at least a year, so he thought it would make good firewood. He trimmed the branches from the log and set them aside for later. He chopped the log into foot-long pieces and put the shavings in a pile. They could use the shavings for kindling. He carried an armful of the wood to the cave with Pepper wagging his tail and following behind.

"You guys, come help me," he said.

"But our hair isn't dry," Luke whined.

"Come anyway, so we'll have some dry wood."

Reluctantly, both of the kids followed Adam out of the cave after he'd piled the wood into a heap near their fire area.

"Luke, get a sack so that you can bring some kindling. I've already got it ready for you."

"Why can't Leila carry the kindling?" he asked.

Exasperated, Adam said, "Just bring a sack, and both of you come with me. Everyone has to do their part. It is the way things are right now."

Quietly, they followed.

Leila was running her fingers through her hair. "I don't have a brush or comb."

Adam felt sorry for her then. She wasn't whining. She just simply stated a fact. The next time he went somewhere, he would look for some things for her hair. He hadn't thought of it before.

By the time they all got back to the cave, they were warmed up, and they opened a can of peaches. Using the can opener was so much easier, and Adam didn't have to worry about ruining his only pocket knife.

He went to the ledge and got the pair of pliers down, along with the small paring knife. He cut off the tops of two pop cans and one beer can. Then he used the pliers to bend over the tops to make a lip so that they could use them for glasses.

"Here you go, you guys, you can now split your pop by pouring half in each glass. The beer can will be my glass. That way, we can keep them straight. You can also use them to get a glass of water."

"Wow!" Luke said. "Those are cool. Where did you get that idea?"

"Do you mean I finally did something that is cool?" Adam asked, smiling.

As it got close to dark, Adam got an empty can, filled it with water, and went down toward the road to gather up some dirt for making mud. He covered the disturbed ground with duff from the forest floor to hide the hole. He went back up to the cave and let some water drip into the can. He stirred it with a stick and made a thick mud. He got three of the potatoes, patted the mud over each potato, and smoothed it out with his hands. The mud didn't stick as well as he thought it would, but he started the fire anyway. When he had good coals, he placed each potato into the little fire and piled the coals on top of them.

He told Leila, "I'm going to watch the potatoes. You get the cheese out of our food can." She quietly did as he asked and didn't ask any questions. Leila was better company than Luke. He felt sorry for her because she had to stay with Luke while Adam was scavenging on his treasure hunts.

When Adam thought the potatoes were done, he raked them out of the fire and let them sit while he got three plates. He knocked off the remaining mud and put each potato on a plate. He then cut some small pieces of cheese and placed them into a slit on each potato. Both kids were observing his every move, and Adam hoped the potatoes would be good. They had been absorbed in the process. The three of them ate their potatoes. Adam noticed there were parts of his potato that weren't quite done, but he ate all of his anyway.

He carefully watched the kids while he ate and noticed that Luke made a face when he got a piece of potato that wasn't quite done, but he kept eating. Adam thought it was amazing how much a person's attitude toward food could change when he was genuinely hungry and knew that food was limited. They were all learning how to survive--one day at a time.

After supper, Leila cleaned everything up, and Adam got his things ready for another trip. This time, he thought he'd walk toward the Indian reservation. Somehow he couldn't see the native people allowing themselves to go to the government and let themselves be part of a work crew. He knew none of them would have papers showing that they were of Latin descent, and the radio had stated that there would no longer be such a thing as a reservation. He had no idea who had deeded land, and who didn't. He finished packing his backpack, and almost as an afterthought, he put two jars of peanut butter and two jars of jelly into his backpack as he got ready for the next day's excursion.

His plan was to find some native people and get them to teach him more about survival. He had no idea how to use the ocean for food, but he knew they would. It was their heritage. Nothing would stop the native people from hiding the same way as Adam. He was sure that at least some of them would hide out--much like his own family had--and he'd find them.

Chapter 14 - Searching For Food

Adam set out early the next morning. "You kids can get something to eat for breakfast and lunch, but eat sparingly, okay?"

They both nodded silently. Adam had boiled some eggs to eat on the way and packed some salt this time. Neither of the kids wanted a boiled egg, which was fine with Adam.

Before he left, he told the kids, "Keep Pepper here with you, and don't worry if I'm not back until late tomorrow. Leila, I'll try my best to find you a brush and comb and some real shampoo."

"Thank you," she answered. "But it is lonesome when you are gone."

"Well, maybe you can work on the cave and play with Pepper, but go no farther than the road. And always duck and hide if you hear a helicopter."

Then he asked Luke, "How is the sore spot on your leg? Let's check it real quick before I go."

Luke walked up to Adam and pulled up his pants leg. Some of the scab had come off, and it was oozing a bit.

"Have you been picking at this?" he asked Luke.

Luke didn't answer. He just nodded his head slightly to indicate a yes.

"The scab is there to keep out germs, okay? Let Pepper lick your leg today and make sure you keep your hands off of the scab, even if it itches a bit. You want it to heal, don't you?" Luke nodded his head yes.

With that, Adam headed out. It was very quiet and barely light enough to see. He hated this time of year because the days were so short. He liked longer days when it didn't rain quite as much. The woods were so quiet that Adam could hear each step. Birds were not yet stirring. He liked it when they made their chirping sounds because it made him feel a little like everything was normal even though nothing at all was really normal--not even the land. He just hoped to hang on, and he hoped that his parents got back to them.

It wasn't long before the birds gave him the comfort he needed. He could hear them, and he relaxed with their chorus of singing. He was starting to recognize some of the different birds. He didn't know anything about birds. He had never been interested in them before. He made up names like "brown bird," "blue bird," and "tiny bird." Maybe he'd find time to learn more about the birds in the area.

He walked on, trying to mentally picture just where the reservation could be found. For the first time, he cut across a large open area where loggers had been clear-cutting. He noted that there was debris from the logging laying all over the ground as he came across a large patch of blackberry vines. He walked around these. He smiled as he remembered the legend he'd heard as a child about Brer Rabbit running from Brer Fox and ducking under the brambles of briars. He wondered if the legend had referred to blackberry vines because they were indigenous to the West Coast. The story of Brer Rabbit reminded him that he needed to keep a good hiding place in mind, so he hurried across the open area toward the woods. Instead of walking down a road, he just cut across the clearing at about a forty-five degree angle.

After he got back among the trees, it was a lot easier to walk because the ground was mostly bare except for some tall trees that were easy to walk around. He tried paying attention to his surroundings, but it was hard. He found his mind wandering back to when things were normal. He wondered what the new normal would be. How long would it take his country to get their act together? Were American troops from around the world being sent back home? What kind of policy for foreign intervention would the new government have for the people? He didn't know.

Adam seemed to get tired all of a sudden, so he stopped under a tree to get a drink of water and eat two of his eggs. They tasted so much better with a little salt, but he knew that even without the salt, he'd eat them anyway. He realized that all three of them had been losing weight, and he was worried about the gash on Luke's leg.

He rubbed his chin--which now had stubble growing. He couldn't do anything about it for the moment, but he could imagine what he might look like to a stranger. He started getting up to continue his quest, when he heard a helicopter. He hugged the tree. He knew he was well-hidden, but he realized he couldn't risk getting into an open area again, especially now that the sun had come out. When the sound of the helicopter disappeared, Adam sat down against the tree in the soft bed of evergreen needles and took a short nap.

After waking up, he got a quick drink of water and took off walking. This time, he walked faster. He was trying to make up some of the time he had lost. He hoped that he would find the reservation before dark. If he didn't find it by then, he'd just have to sleep in the understory of a thick grove of trees and hope that he didn't intrude on any bears or other large animals. Adam knew there were coyotes in these woods, but so far he had not seen any of them. He still had two eggs that he'd intended to eat the next morning. But he decided that the pungent smell of the eggs could draw coyotes or bears, so he dug out both eggs, put one in his pocket, and peeled the other one as he walked. He dug out the salt, salted the egg, and kept on walking. Then he did the same with the other egg. They were gone.

Just as the daylight began getting dimmer and fog started crowding into the low areas, Adam saw a couple of old buildings. He thought that they might be on the edge of the reservation, but he decided to check them out. He stopped to listen for any sign of life. He heard only birds.

He moved carefully from tree to tree, edging closer to the two buildings. One building looked like it had been constructed to serve as a garage for machinery or a car. Car tracks led up to the garage, but no type of automobile was visible. He worked his way up to the building and peeked inside. The inside was dark, so Adam had to concentrate to focus his vision. He listened. He peered. He stepped forward.

Then, he saw it. A boat. A large boat. He put out his hands and touched the boat, running his fingers down the bottom. The boat was still on a boat trailer. It was still wet with moisture dripping under it. He looked inside and saw that a small amount of water rested just under the seat. That water was not old, moldy water that was full of algae. It was fresh out of the ocean. He heard a sound, then jumped slightly before he froze. He listened again but couldn't hear anything.

Adam had the feeling that someone was outside. He crouched

behind the boat and waited, not knowing what he waited for or why. He was motionless and a little bit apprehensive. Would whoever was outside come in? He wasn't sure. He couldn't decide what to do. He tried to remember how long it had been since the helicopter had flown over the woods. He had not heard a helicopter since that time, and it had been several hours. No, he decided, it wasn't the helicopter men. He still waited, feeling his heart pumping hard. His whole body was in hyper-alert status. Again, he listened and only heard what he perceived as the thud of his own heart.

It seemed to be a stalemate with someone outside the garage and him inside. Both hiding. Both cautious. Both conditioned to be fearful. More than an hour passed. Adam heard nothing more, yet he still sensed that something or someone was just outside going through the same fear as him.

Finally, Adam decided to just get it over with. He went to the door of the garage and yelled out, "I don't know who you are, but I'm hiding from the helicopter people too."

Then he remembered his peanut butter and jelly. "I have brought food to share, and I mean no harm to anyone." He stood still and listened. Then he added, "I'd like to meet you because maybe we can help each other. I have no intention of becoming a part of this new Democratic Latin Alliance. I'm not paying them one cent, and neither is my family."

That last statement had been an afterthought, and Adam realized that he had really stuck his neck out with that one. If whoever he heard did happen to be one of the helicopter men, he had probably got himself into one heap of trouble. He waited near the entrance of the garage. After what seemed like several minutes, he heard footsteps approaching him. He crouched down and tried to prepare himself to either fight or run away, or some combination of the two. The footsteps came around the corner of the garage, and Adam saw the source of his fear come into view. He was surprised to see another guy his own age. He had a vague familiarity. There he was. A guy he remembered from high school. They had both played basketball--Adam for Shelton High School and the other guy for Aberdeen High School. Adam tried to remember his name. They had talked many times and liked each other. The two guys, both shocked, stood staring at each other.

Reaching out his hand tentatively, Adam said, "Adam Bennett."

The other guy took Adam's hand, shaking it as he said, "Caleb Graywolf."

The two boys sat down against the outside wall of the building and began talking.

Adam said, "My family and I planned to hide out in a cave, but the earthquake separated us. Now I'm stuck with my younger brother and sister, and we don't even know if our parents are alive"

Caleb glanced at Adam and told him, "Our family has been hiding out ever since the Democratic Latin Alliance took over. Then the earthquake hit. We've been short of food, but we're making it. Come on, I'll introduce you to the rest of my family. There are a few more families here, but they won't come out to meet you. We fear everyone these days. The way we see it, that is how we will survive. If I hadn't already known you, I would never have come out of hiding. In fact, my parents just might be angry at me, but we'll see. Do you still want to come with me?"

"I'd love to meet the rest of your family. You and I have always gotten along, and I see no reason why we shouldn't get along now. Who knows, maybe we can help each other. We are all against the new government."

"That is where you are wrong."

"What do you mean?"

Caleb looked at Adam like he couldn't believe he didn't understand. He tried to explain. "The Democratic Latin Alliance declared an end to the reservations. Some people thought this might be a good thing. Those families are on the mainland now."

"I can't believe it!" Adam said, shaking his head back and forth.

"After the earthquake, we made a few trips to the mainland to get some food that we don't have. The others seem to feel they are doing okay, but I'm not sure. I just don't want to be anyone's slave."

Adam was solemn and spoke softly, "I don't want to be anyone's slave either, but I also don't want to starve. What a dilemma!"

"We can always go back to the mainland before starving, but we'll put up a hell of a fight first. Let's go. You can meet my family."

"Let's go. Is your Mom a good cook?"

"The best. But, of course, she doesn't have much to work with these days."

The boys stood up and began slowly walking deeper into the

woods. They didn't talk. They just walked. Each boy was concentrating on his own thoughts and problems. They walked for about two hours, then Adam saw a small house. Adam had found some other people.

Chapter 15 - The Reservation

Caleb saw the look of surprise on Adam's face and felt the need to explain. "This is not where we've always lived, but we moved here because it is more hidden than our real house."

They were gazing at a little one-roomed, summer-type cabin built with logs. It had an A-frame style roof and was barely visible, even close up.

"How clever," Adam said. The cabin had been built of roughhewn logs that were probably logged from fairly close by. The door was made from rough lumber that had been handmade.

"There are others," Caleb said. "They are scattered around--not all grouped together. Sometimes we get together, but we do it very carefully and only with lookouts posted."

The two boys entered the cabin. At first, it appeared that there was no one present.

"Mom, Dad, I have brought someone." There was complete silence. No one stirred, even though both boys were aware that there was someone in the cabin.

Caleb spoke again, "Mom, Adam is here with me, and we were friends before. He is hiding out too. He has brought us something."

With that last comment, Caleb's mother climbed down from the loft. "Caleb, I can't believe you brought someone here," she said. She seemed hostile to Adam, but he really couldn't blame her.

Caleb said, "Mom, this is Adam Bennett. He played on the basketball team for Shelton, and we were always friends. He is okay. He means us no harm. He is not a part of the new government."

Adam pulled off his backpack, pulled out the two jars of peanut butter and the two jars of jelly, and handed them to Mrs. Graywolf.

"Here, we don't have any form of bread, and can't use the jelly. We have only one box of crackers left, but we have more peanut butter."

He set the jars on the table. "Our parents got separated from us because of the earthquake, so we don't even know if they are alive. I thought maybe you guys could help me learn more about how to eat off the land. We would rather not starve. I am trying to take care of a younger brother and sister," he said. He looked at Mrs. Graywolf and found himself holding his breath.

Adam had appealed to the mother in Mrs. Graywolf. She answered him almost in a whisper, "Adam, are you hungry?"

"Well, I ate hard-boiled eggs for breakfast and again for lunch, but now that you mention food, I could sure eat!"

Smiling and looking at Adam, Caleb said, "Thanks, Mom. I think we could both eat."

Mrs. Graywolf offered Adam some hot coffee and gave him a tortilla on a plate. Then she put a crock-type container on the table. She had used pot holders to take the pot out of the fireplace.

"Here, you put beans on top of the tortilla and roll it up. We think it is real good."

Adam did as she instructed him. Beans fell out of the bottom, with the juice following. Caleb was getting himself some tortilla and beans too.

"Here's what you do. You put the beans only in the middle, then you fold up the bottom, and roll up your tortilla. That way, the beans don't fall out."

As he talked, he demonstrated for Adam, who followed his lead after unrolling his tortilla. Sure enough, it worked! The beans didn't fall out. Adam ate hungrily.

"This is the best thing I've eaten for a very long time, Mrs. Graywolf. Thank you so much!"

She looked at Adam with a slow smile, which grew larger and larger. "Just what do you have to eat?" she asked.

"Peanut butter and crackers, and some macaroni. We've eaten most of the eggs and not much else. We do have some canned foods too. We have some canned peaches and some canned chili."

"Do you have any kind of bread?"

"No, and that makes it hard to eat something like peanut butter or jelly."

"Would you like a sack of flour?"

"I wouldn't know what to do with flour. I remember my mother making biscuits, but she used an oven. All we have is a fire, and we keep that low so that it won't smoke."

"I'll tell you what. I'll show you how to make tortillas, and you can use them with your chili and peanut butter. Would that help?"

"Oh, my, the kids would think that they died and went to heaven," he told her, chuckling.

Caleb was so grateful to his mother, he got up from his chair and gave her a hug. Adam could see there was an easy affection between them, and for the first time, Adam realized that he'd never really had that kind of relationship with his own mother.

"Let's make a batch of tortillas right now!" Mrs. Graywolf suggested.

"You're on!" Adam said, grinning.

Mrs. Graywolf got a bowl and filled it about a third of the way with flour. "Help Adam get washed up because he's going to do this-- with our help."

She got out some baking powder, a large can of lard, and a box of salt.

Then she told Adam, "Use about this much flour," as she tipped the bowl. "Use about a half teaspoon of salt and about two teaspoons of baking powder. Give it a stir, then put in a large pat of lard. Mix it into the flour with a fork, like this."

Mrs. Graywolf handed him the fork. He mixed, conscious that everyone was watching him, until he could hardly tell the lard was in the flour at all. He looked at Mrs. Graywolf with a questioning expression on his face. She handed him a large spoon and told him to make a well in the center of the bowl of flour, then handed him the spoon. He took it and concentrated on making the well.

"Okay, Adam, you pour a little water in--about a half cup--then stir it together. The big trick is to stir the flour mixture minimally after you add the water because overworking makes your dough tough. Just give it a few stirs, and you can tell how much water you might need to add."

She took the spoon from him, pushed the wet dough together

on one side, and added more water. She dampened the rest of the mix, pushed it all together, and picked up the whole ball with her hands. Then she put flour on a countertop and kneaded the ball of dough. She made little balls with the dough--each about the size of a lime--and patted the dough back and forth from one hand to the other until it was flat and round. She handed the rounded dough to Adam and asked Caleb to put the large cast iron skillet on the side of the fire. They waited for it to get hot.

Mrs. Graywolf took the round piece of dough and put a small amount of lard in the skillet. She tossed in the tortilla and watched until little bubbles came to the surface. She turned the tortilla over with the spoon and browned the other side.

"Get your plate, Adam," she commanded. He shoved the plate toward her, and she plopped the tortilla onto the plate and said, "It tastes the best when it is still warm--right after it is cooked. We make a whole batch at one time, and keep them covered to eat later. They'll keep a couple of days. If you make tortillas, you will be able to feed those kids better, and you will then be able to use your peanut butter and jelly."

Adam was munching on the tortilla. She was already making another one, which Caleb quickly claimed. Adam was full for the first time in a long time and it made him sleepy. "Mrs. Graywolf, can I just sleep inside with you guys? I'll sleep on the floor. I'm used to it."

A man burst inside the cabin, walked toward Mrs. Graywolf, then stopped frozen and stared at Adam. That was when Adam realized that this, then, was Caleb's dad, Mr. Graywolf.

"Where did he come from?" He nodded toward Adam in a very unfriendly manner. Caleb introduced Adam to his dad and explained his situation. His reception was still frosty. Mrs. Graywolf told him that Adam would spend the night, then leave in the morning.

"But then he'll know where we live and can tell those others." He did not care that Adam was standing right there.

Mrs. Graywolf told him, "No, he won't because he has two kids to take care of, and his hands are full as it is."

By then, Mr. Graywolf had gotten some coffee and a tortilla. He put some beans on top and folded it the way Caleb had showed Adam.

Mrs. Graywolf told Adam, "If you sort of mash up the beans a bit, they go on the tortilla a lot easier and they will be easier for the kids to manage."

"Thank you, Mrs. Graywolf, that sounds like a great idea. Mr. Graywolf, it was nice to meet you." He held out his hand, but Mr. Graywolf didn't take it. He just kept eating.

Mr. and Mrs. Graywolf climbed to the loft. Caleb stayed back with Adam. Mr. Graywolf had not said one thing to him. He watched as the two Graywolfs went up the ladder. The two boys lay down on the floor in front of the little fire. Adam hoped they didn't hear a helicopter on this particular night. It had been a long, stressful day for him. The boys discussed how they had survived after the earthquake. Their conversation turned toward the new government and what it meant. They continued talking in hushed voices until they finally fell asleep.

Neither boy awakened until it began to get light outside. They both went outside to get fresh air and to check out the surroundings. When they came back to the cabin, Mr. Graywolf was chopping wood.

Adam went over to the small pile of wood and asked, "Would you like me to carry this wood inside for you?" He had decided not to give the man any choice but to talk to him.

Mr. Graywolf acted surprised. "Why sure, son," he answered. Caleb had gone inside the house and returned with a basket that he was now putting the wood chips into.

All three of the guys went into the house at the same time--to the smell of fresh coffee which Mrs. Graywolf had made. Adam had never been much of a coffee drinker, but it sure smelled good that morning. The Graywolfs sat down at the table and ate a tortilla with jelly on it while they drank their coffee. None of the Graywolfs were talkative, but Adam found he rather enjoyed the quiet calm in their home. He sensed an easy camaraderie between the family members. He could see so many differences between their family and his own, and it made him a little sad to think about what he'd missed.

Adam smiled at Mr. Graywolf. "How do you like the jelly?"

"I love it. I like the peanut butter too." Mr. Graywolf gave a little nudge toward Adam with the plate of tortillas. Adam picked up one, put jelly on it, and rolled it up like Caleb had shown him the night before.

"You are right. Tortillas really are good with the jelly. The kids would love this." He thought about Luke and Leila and knew they didn't have anything quite as good to eat for breakfast.

"Mrs. Graywolf, did you mean what you said about giving me some flour and baking powder?"

"I sure did," she said. "And how about the lard. Do you have any lard?"

"No, I don't," he told her." I do have some butter, but it is old."

"If you have any potatoes, you can chop one up and cook it in bad grease. Somehow the potato will absorb the rancid taste and smell right out of the grease. You will have nice fresh grease then."

"I had no idea," he said. "That will be a big help. After breakfast, would you show me how to cook beans?   We do have beans."

Mr. Graywolf answered, "Mom makes great beans. She just puts into them whatever we have. This jelly tortilla tastes so good this morning. We can give you some lard, Adam. We can spare some. It will be good for the kids too. Put a little meat on them."

Mrs. Graywolf smiled. "We have a lot of lard because just two weeks ago a whale beached himself, and we got to work quickly to make it into lard. The fat was divided, and we had as much as we could carry and store. We'll give you some."

"Will it make tortillas this good?"

"There is nothing like whale grease for making and cooking tortillas."

It was noon by the time Adam finally left, and he found himself a little reluctant to leave. "Caleb, do you want to go with me and see where I am staying?"

Adam didn't really think Caleb would come with him. He was just trying to prolong leaving.

"I'd like that if Mom and Dad don't need me for anything."

His dad told him, "Go ahead. Then you'll know where he stays. You can help pack the whale lard for him and meet his brother and sister."

Adam was surprised, but pleased. The two boys left with a couple of tortillas each, a sack of flour, and baking powder in Adam's pack. Caleb packed the lard. Both boys were loaded down for trekking through the woods, but they were also looking forward to the adventure. They set out with Adam in the lead.

Chapter 16 - The Homecoming

Adam and Caleb walked for a long time in silence. Then they stopped and listened to the sound of the woods. They leaned up against a tall tree that was large enough for both of them. They had not heard a helicopter since they left the Graywolf house, and both of the guys were glad about this.

They took out two tortillas, rolled them up, and ate as slowly as they could. "You know, Caleb, your mother was right. These are almost as good cold."

Caleb answered him, "You got that right."

"I'm a little bit envious about how easily you get along with your parents. I've never gotten along with my own parents, and I've never known why."

"I've just always thought our family was just a normal family."

"I guess I've just never felt like I was part of a family." Adam confided to his new friend.

"That is too bad! Do you think it is because your brother and sister are so much younger than you?"

"I don't know. I just don't know. Let's go. Maybe after you meet my brother and sister, you can give me an idea."

"Gee, Adam, I'd hate to say anything about your family. If I can think of any ideas that are constructive, I'll tell you. Otherwise, I probably won't say a thing."

"Let's go. We're just about two hours away. And after we get there, I have exactly one beer left. I'll split it with you. Won't that taste good?"

Caleb answered him, "You bet."

They walked beside each other in silence, each one thinking their own thoughts. The afternoon bird serenades were beginning. It brought Adam pleasure, as usual, to hear them. It made the surroundings seem normal even though there was nothing normal at all. The birds were the only thing that seemed to be the way they should be. The government wasn't normal. It wasn't normal for little kids to be stranded away from their parents. It wasn't normal to not be able to get home when you felt like it. It wasn't normal for Caleb and his family to live in a cabin deep in the woods. And it wasn't normal for Adam to be living in a cave. Only the birds still had "normal."

"We turn off here," Adam said to Caleb. "It is up that mountain."

"You sure can't see it from the road," Caleb said. "I think that is in your favor. What is it like, anyway, living in a cave?"

"You will soon find out," Adam said.

As they got closer to the cave, he got a strange feeling that something was wrong. Pepper was barking, but Adam expected that. All of the normal mountain sounds were gone. Adam could feel a prickly feeling of fear running up his spine. He motioned to Caleb to step aside, and he ducked into the cave as fast as he could. When Pepper recognized him, he quit barking and wagged his tail as he ran to him.

When Adam entered the cave, he sensed that someone else was there. After a moment, his eyes adjusted enough for him to see his mom and dad standing near the back of the cave.

"So you are alive!" he said. His heart beat hard with joy and excitement. It seemed like it had been a long time since he had known he still had parents. He yelled for Caleb, "Come on in, Caleb. It is my mom and dad."

Just as Caleb stepped into the cave and Adam was about to introduce his parents to him, he noticed his beer. His dad's hand was circled around Adam's last beer. He'd even already opened it. His dad took a sip!

"Dad! You opened my last beer without even asking me? Caleb and I were going to split it."

"Since when is this YOUR beer?" His father yelled. Adam got angry so fast that he kicked the side of the cave and hurt his foot--again.

"Dad, you and Mom have been gone for almost two weeks. Where have you been?"

111

Caleb stood there looking uncomfortable. "Adam, do you think I should leave?"

"No! Please, no!"

"If you'd been taking care of your brother and sister instead of playing around with friends, you would already know the answer to that. We couldn't get back right after the earthquake."

"Where is my car?" Adam asked.

"It is gone, and so is our house. We barely escaped with our lives. We came back for all of you. We are living in the family camp, and we came by boat to get you."

Adam had a comb and brush that Mrs. Graywolf had given him for Leila, and he told her, "I didn't forget about your comb and brush, but if you leave, you won't need these."

Leila smiled at Adam and said, "Thank you, Adam."

Adam's dad said, "What do you mean 'if?'"

"I don't think I'm going back with you," Adam told him.

"You don't have a choice," his dad said.

You forget that I'm 18 now, and I don't have to do everything you think up for me to do."

The cave suddenly seemed to be stifling, and Adam felt crowded. He glanced at Caleb. "I'm staying here. I'm not staying in a camp run by that new government."

Adam's mom spoke up, "Adam, you can't stay here in this squalor!"

"Mom, I've worked hard to take care of the kids--in spite of what Dad thinks--and I'm not going back until the United States is back in control."

"That may be never," his dad said. "And what if you starve?"

"Then I'll starve by my own actions," he said.

"In that case, we'll be taking the kids and going."

His dad began picking up the kids' things, which they had already packed. They set Adam's things aside. Luke ran to Adam and wrapped his arms around him. "But, Adam, you can't stay here by yourself."

Then, he acknowledged Caleb. "Hi."

Adam told Luke, "This is Caleb."

Then Leila ran to Adam and told him sympathetically, "You took good care of us, and I know it was probably hard. I tried to help."

"You did help. More than you'll ever know. I'll miss you, Leila."

"You can't stay here by yourself," she said. She was about to cry.

Adam's mom looked at Adam holding Leila and said, "I really wish you would come back with us. I'll be worried about you if you don't."

His dad said, "I'll be back to get you in two weeks. By then, you'll be ready to come back to the mainland. Let's go!" He didn't look back.

Xander, Claire, Luke, and Leila left the cave with their backpacks full. Caleb and Adam walked with them as far as the road. They watched the group as they slowly walked down the road. Luke and Leila waved back at them. Adam's parents didn't even look back or thank Adam for taking such good care of the kids. In fact, they probably thought he'd done a terrible job. His dad, as usual, was angry with him. He always had gotten angry so easily.

Adam was glad his parents were alive. He knew he'd miss Luke and Leila. It seemed like Luke had changed a lot since all of this happened. Adam felt like he'd probably still worry about them. He'd especially worry about Leila. He wanted her to get to go to school. He cuddled Pepper in his arms as he and Caleb walked back up to the now almost empty cave. It seemed a comfort for him to be holding Pepper. He was glad he had him.

They had left the cave a mess, and Adam began straightening up. "We'll have a can of chili and a can of peaches for supper, Caleb. You are going to spend the night, aren't you?"

"Of course."

"I'm really glad because it is going to be very different without the kids. Most everything I did was to take care of them. I won't have the incentive to work quite as hard now."

The kids had left the bedding, so Adam and Caleb put together a bedroll for themselves after they ate. Adam rolled up Caleb's bedroll and lay on his own. He couldn't help but ponder the new quiet. To Adam, it seemed too quiet. Here, all of this time, he'd thought he wanted more quiet, but now he wasn't so sure. He was glad to have Caleb and Pepper for company.

He'd get the Graywolfs to teach him about getting clams, oysters, and fish out of the ocean--how to use the ocean for food. He knew that he would soon run out of things to scavenge. He cuddled the little dog in his arms as he went to sleep. He wasn't much in the mood for conversation.

The next morning, Adam boiled four eggs, and shared them with Caleb. They tasted good. Caleb got ready to go back to his cabin, and Adam waved at him from the cave opening. "Come back, Caleb," he said.

"I will."

Then, Adam went back inside the cave, rolled up Caleb's bedroll, and lay down on his bedroll. He'd keep that for Caleb.

He was alone. At last. And it was quiet. Stone quiet. Pepper snuggled up against him, and they both lay there listening to the forest sounds. It felt good, but it also felt lonely. Thank goodness he had the Graywolfs. Adam suddenly had a new life. His life was in his own hands. His world was changing, and maybe it wouldn't be the world he really wanted. It was too quiet.

Would his father return in two weeks? What would he tell his father when and if he did return for him? He didn't know. For now, he'd gotten what he'd wished for: no kids. So far, he didn't really like it.

--#--